24 HOURS WITH GASPAR

SEAGULL
BOOKS
•
CELEBRATING
40 YEARS

SABDA ARMANDIO

24 HOURS WITH GASPAR

Translated from the Indonesian by
LARA NORGAARD

With illustrations by
RADITYO WICAKSONO

LONDON NEW YORK CALCUTTA

Seagull Books, 2023

Originally published in Indonesian as *24 Jam Bersama Gaspar*
by Buku Mojok, Ngaglik, Yogyakarta, Indonesia

© Sabda Armandio, 2017

First published in English translation by Seagull Books, 2023
English translation © Lara Norgaard, 2023

Illustrations courtesy Radityo Wicaksono

ISBN   978 1 80309 2 041

British Library Cataloguing-in-Publication Data
A catalogue record for this book is available from the British Library

Typeset at Seagull Books, Calcutta, India
Printed and bound in the USA by Versa Press

24 HOURS WITH GASPAR

FOREWORD

Before we parted ways in the courtyard of the Gberia Fotombu Mosque, an Arab traveller who had befriended me over the course of more than 1,001 nights gave me the following advice: 'Remember, my friend, nothing is so dangerous as stories that have you believe good always triumphs over evil, as they will make you dim-witted and cruel.'

He entered the mosque and I continued walking towards Makeni. Recalling how he'd never run out of tales the entire time we'd spent together there in Sierra Leone, I believed his words held some truth. But later, in the hull of a minecart heading to Pepel, I began to wonder if he'd fed me empty digressions. As we all know, all stories that human beings tell leave us with an instructive message so that the next generation will continue to believe that evil is evil without having to go to the trouble of bothering themselves over moral dilemmas. And who's daft enough to write about the rise of evil? If such people exist, their stories wouldn't last very long at all.

I was wrong. One afternoon, a few years after saying farewell to that storyteller, I met an 18-year-old girl who reminded me of his message. She began her anecdote with a simple question: 'Have you ever heard of the crime of March 4th?'

Indonesia is familiar with dates tied to tragedies: 12 May, four students killed; 28 June, the Mandor Affair; 12 September, the Tanjung Priok Massacre; 22 October, a pilot in training crashes a fighter jet into the National Monument; and lastly, the most widely known date, debated to no end: the 30th of September Movement, 1965. Or the ill-fated day humanity will never forget: 27 December, the Day of Conception. Though I was well aware of all these stories, the peculiar crime of March 4th was new to me.

The girl heard about the March 4th incident from her mother, who'd in turn heard it from her grandmother. Recounting the tale to new acquaintances was also a family tradition, she told me. Unfortunately, a robot server interrupted her by spilling coffee on her dress and she went to the restroom to wash out the stain. We were at a little cafe at Pantai Margonda in the Depok neighbourhood of Jakarta. The manager apologized. Please understand, this sort of thing tends to happen, the robot's imported, second-hand. When my new friend returned to her seat, the city alarm sounded and the chip inserted into the back of my right hand blinked.

'I'll finish another time,' she said. 'I have to get back to work.'

2

'There might not be another time.' I asked if I could meet her mother.

'You're really curious, aren't you?' Without waiting for me to respond, she placed a finger to her lips and then pressed a glowing pink symbol on her neck.

After a momentary silence, she spoke. 'I just told Mom. She says you can come over this afternoon.'

She flicked her wrist in the air as she announced the address, and instantly a virtual screen the size of Paul Klee's *Cat and Bird* stretched out in front of us. A red dot flashed above the location. Plucking the screen from the air, she held out her hand to pass the screen over to me, but I hadn't installed the necessary update in my body yet. 'Could you sketch it out instead?'

After grumbling and lecturing me about the importance of technology for the elderly, she pulled a 3D pen from her pocket to create a detailed map, exactly like the one on the screen, and then handed me the mini diorama. 'How about you draw it on paper?' I said. 'That way, I can keep it in my wallet. I won't lose it.'

More grumbling as she grabbed a standard pen and napkin, then wrote out the directions. 'Take this street here. Look for the green house.'

*

Notes in hand, I made my way to the address. Though the girl's mom had died five years earlier, her consciousness had been uploaded into a robot body with a tube-shaped head and a torso cluttered with silly refrigerator magnets—inside, red and blue cables were hooked up to a fresh brain soaking in fluid. The creature emitted sounds through mouth-like speakers. Her iron hands each looked like the arm of a desk lamp, and she rolled about on tank treads.

The humanoid disclosed what she knew about the incident. When I mentioned the name Gaspar, she seemed upset; there was a glitch in her voice and a quivering of grey matter. I began to suspect that the woman and Gaspar had once been connected. I gathered leads for a few other people to talk to, including a patient at Marzuki Mahdi Hospital in Bogor.

This man was not like the other patients. He was elderly and refused to wear the required white hospital gown. Instead, he had donned a grey button-down and a hat that he purportedly only removed in the shower. His front teeth were chipped, and he insisted on telling me why before I asked a single question. The man had been deemed perfectly healthy 30 years earlier, but he'd refused to leave the hospital because, as we all know, the Conception Programme sometimes caused trauma. According to his doctor, the hospital let him stay on the condition that he work for room and board. He was strong, despite his age. He owned a few dozen copies of the book *Soeharto: My Ideas, Speeches, and Actions*, each volume riddled with marginalia. The patient gave me the recording of an interview he'd conducted with a witness of the March 4th Incident. He'd been waiting a long time for someone like me to come along, he said.

I'm aware that the adventures of Gaspar and his friends might seem odd to you. The city where the incident took place is now underwater, the modes of transportation that appear throughout may be difficult to imagine, and the outdated terms I employ seem primitive and silly today. Nevertheless, the emotions at the heart of the story—fear, anxiety, sadness—persist across time, as do our distinctions between good and bad, which, having remained unquestioned, still carry about them that same absolute quality. It appears that the Conception Programme was created in vain; human beings will always find a way to be fools. I believe it's important that my contemporaries hear Gaspar's story, so that we do not continue to be so dim-witted and cruel.

Armed with interviews from dozens of sources and a worn-out copy of *My Days*, I've strung together the story of Gaspar into 22 chapters. The volume you hold in your hands now has a mere eight, but that should suffice to grasp the essence of Gaspar's story and apply it today, so that you can find a way to change things (surely, you know what I'm referring to). I've attached transcripts of an interview with a witness to the events, even though some sections of audio—the openings and a few brief segments in the middle of the conversations—are damaged. My rationale is that you might find important messages in these documents, or at least I believe you can. And, of course, discovering them on your own, without my help, will be more meaningful.

One of my sources compared Gaspar to a little centipede that lives in your ear: you can feel its tiny legs perpetually awriggle, hear its constant whispers. At first, I thought the comparison was hyperbolic—that is, until my own investigation into Gaspar required me to descend deep into his circle of hell. Assuming Gaspar's perspective left me disgusted with myself.

Allow me to conclude my introduction with a message from the aforementioned patient: each year, on the fourth of March, symbols of truth lose their meaning, the desires buried within us rise to the surface, and those clever enough to recognize what's happening strike a match and toss it into whatever might look beautiful ablaze.

Regards,
Artur Harahap

VN 4F1F

The humanoid enjoys greeting her neighbours through speakers embedded in her chest. Husni, a woman who lives next door, frequently travels abroad and makes sure to bring back fridge magnets as souvenirs for VN 4F 1F.

01

My name is Gaspar, I'm 35 years old.

I'm the one big dragons tell stories about when they want their kiddie dragons to go to bed: 'You better—or else he'll come and get you.' Kim Il-sung used to howl out my name and all the terrible things that I'm capable of doing to make little Kim Jong-il stop whining. I'm savage, I won't deny it; but still, I can't resist a brainy detective like Sherlock Holmes. Holmes cracks me up. I mean, what's funny about him are his faculties of deductive reasoning: each problem he solves has about fifty plausible explanations, and if readers really put their minds to it, all of his twaddle becomes dry comedy. When I was 24, back when I used to write, I came up with a short story about a famous detective who always got things wrong because he was a fanatic for truth, exactly like those zealots during the Inquisition who translated Luke 14:23 literally. But Holmes has his followers, and in their eyes, he's never wrong. I dedicated that story of mine to Holmes, but the dedication could have applied just as easily to Poirot or Miss Marple or Bruce Wayne or their fans.

If you become my friend, I'll have no qualms whatsoever about annihilating your enemies. All you have to do is follow one simple rule: never sneak up on me from behind.

—TRANSCRIPT I—

[Static for 30 seconds]

—n good physical and spiritual health and willin—[static for several seconds]—ightforward explanation of what took place?

Yes and no. As far as my physical health goes, my hip is a bit sore, but that's an old injury. My soul, though, is in excellent working order, inshallah, or at least I've worked hard to—[static for several seconds]—ough I don't know if I fully believe that. I had the sneaking suspicion that I'd met the young man before. The face was familiar, but I couldn't place him. Maybe it was just a bit of déjà vu.

Do you understand why you've been called in to give a statement?

Sort of. What Mr Mustache over there said is that, so far, I'm the only witness the police were able to locate. Everyone else is still on the run. Do you think I'm telling the truth?

That's beside the point. We're following procedure. I'm going to ask you a few questions about the body we found this morning. Are you willing to cooperate?

It's certainly best that I do. Many hands make light work.

All right. At 10 a.m., someone called in to report a nasty smell coming from the neighbour's house. The front gate was locked, the yard was a mess. When we arrived on the scene, the victim's corpse was decomposing on the bed, no signs of foul play. Meanwhile, forensics indicated a heart attack as cause of death, roughly three days ago. But when I got to the scene, I had a hunch it was murder. Just so you know, my intuition is rarely wrong. According to the neighbours, you and your friends were the last to be seen with the victim. The caller identified you—said you're a doctor and wrote them a prescription some time ago. I need an account of your whereabouts over the past four days.

You're right that I used to be a doctor. I had my own practice. I ran it from my house, but that was long ago, and I'm afraid I'm not nearly so well known any more. If I saw the face of whoever called this in, I might recognize who it is. I have a pretty good memory. Wait, is the caller still alive?

Of course. What kind of question is that?

Oh, if they were dead, I could easily identify the body. I never forget the face of someone who dies in front of me.

Every now and again, when I'm minding my own business, those faces pop into my head. But let me see, what was I doing four days ago . . . first, I woke up. Then, after dawn prayers, I fed Jenifer.

Jenifer?

Our pet finch. Actually, she's my husband's bird. She sings marvellously. Oh my, how can I explain it? Have you ever heard a bamboo flute, sir? Well, imagine if the musician only hit the high notes. That's what it sounds like. Sometimes she makes me think of Nike Ardilla, sometimes Nicky Astria. Once, I tried to make my husband change the bird's name to Nike, but he refused. Jenifer is better, he said. I didn't understand what was so good about the name Jenifer, but I just stayed quiet, you know. Dishonour to one's husband—

Enough about Jenifer. What did you do next?

Listen, sir, my memory is good, but I'll lose track of the story if I can't describe what happened in order. If you want me to be clear, please don't interrupt, that's how my mind works. Or else everything will get mixed up and I'll have to start over from the beginning.

Fine. Tell me what you were doing that morning, four days ago.

When I finished praying, I fed Jenifer. Like I said, she's our pet finch—well, my husband's—and she has a lovely voice, like the high notes on a bamboo flute. It reminds me of Nike Ardilla. Oh, Nicky Astria too. Did I mention that I tried to convince my husband to change the bird's name to Nike? He didn't want to, he thought Jenifer was better. What's so great about the name Jenifer? That's what I thought, but I kept quiet. Like my Quran teacher used to say, dishonouring one's husband is the path to hell. Now that I think about it, my husband did explain why he wanted to stick with Jenifer. Your memory might be sharp, but mine's getting weaker, that's what he said. If we went and changed the name, I'd probably forget and start calling her Jenifer again. And if that happened, it'd be bad for the finch, poor thing. Two names? That's confusing. *Who am I, really?* the bird would think and get depressed. Anxious birds die young. Not just birds, we also used to have two rabbits. They were dirty, so I washed them, and then they died, both of them, one right after the other. My friend—she's a veterinarian—says rabbits don't live for very long. Any animal can die from stress. Then I started thinking, what could put an animal into such a state? With people, it's not so hard to imagine. We feel anxious when we can't put food on the table, when our bank accounts run dry, when we can't pay our bills. But animals? Judging from our pets, animals grow distressed when they're bathed or surprised or moved from one place to another, especially if it's somewhere they don't belong. I have no clue if confusion about a name would set a bird on edge. The risk was simply too great, and we weren't ready to lose another pet. Two months ago our goldfish passed away from loneliness. That sort of thing wouldn't happen to, say, a Siamese fighting fish. They're strong.

Sir, I hope you understand why I go a bit overboard with Jenifer. Life has taught me many things about love and loss, life and death. And even though I understand this is the natural order of things, I'm willing to dote on Jenifer all morning in order to delay her departure from this world. It's not as though preparing her food is easy, sir. The only thing Jenifer eats in the morning is porridge—she'll refuse worms if you give them to her. As it turns out, we ran out of corn four days ago, so I headed to the vegetable market for a fresh crate.

You went to the market?

That's right.

At roughly what time?

I don't know. The point is, after finishing dawn prayers and realizing we were out of corn, I rushed to the market. I was just a few steps out the door when I heard the call to prayer from the mosque. So, I went back inside and prayed again.

And you went to the market after that?

No. Don't guess what happened, okay? I was hungry. I decided to buy chicken porridge from the street vendor at the corner, at the far end of my block.

Did the porridge seller see you?

Oh, no, sir. That's not at all what happened. I went to the intersection, but he wasn't there. Maybe it was earlier than I thought.

Is that when you went to the market?

What for?

You said you needed corn for Jenifer.

I did *leave* for the vegetable market, but I never got there. Like I told you, I was on the way but I went back home when the call to prayer started. Look, you have to pay attention when someone is talking to you.

So, you never made it to the vegetable market?

I thought, why bother? I have a cell phone. My son taught me how to call the market, the grocery store, and a few of my neighbours. I don't have the number for the police because my son says cops are too simple to help someone as complex as me. What do you mean 'simple'? That's what I asked him. Straightforward, he said. All you have to do is hand them some cash. They're not interested in your stories. Personally, I don't think the police are as simple as that. You're a good example, sir, because you're listening to me. You're a good officer, not at all like the ones my son goes on about. If you stopped your annoying habit of interrupting people, I'm sure you could be Policeman of the Year.

Who answered the phone when you called the market?

An employee, obviously. I remember his voice: a bit raspy and full of character, like Bob Tutupoly's. If he answers the phone, I get my order in less than half an hour. But if that lazy-sounding woman answers—her voice is like Vina Panduwinata's—that's when the delivery will take closer to an hour. And if it's the little kid who picks up, the one who always seems sleepy, my order won't come at all, and eventually I'll forget all about the vegetables until the next morning when I check Jenifer's corn crate and see that it's empty.

Would you mind calling the market now?

Not at all.

—END OF AUDIO FILE—

BUDI ALAZON

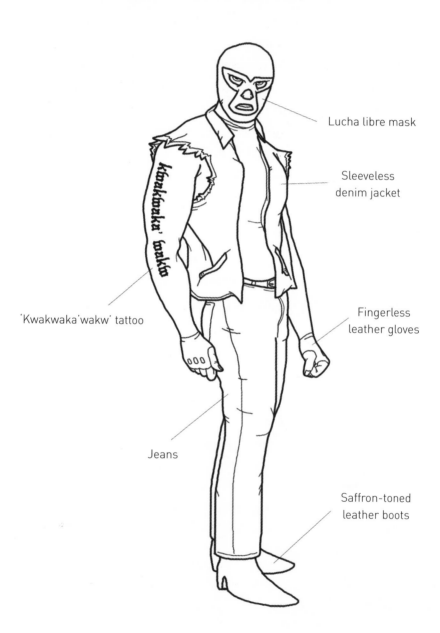

Lucha libre mask

Sleeveless
denim jacket

'Kwakwaka'wakw' tattoo

Fingerless
leather gloves

Jeans

Saffron-toned
leather boots

02

I'm going to rob the jewellery store with help from Cortázar. T minus 24 hours.

I eased off the fuel and Cortázar coasted to a stop by the warung near the store in question. I bought a bottle of iced green tea, a pack of cigarettes and two bars of soap at 12 on the dot. I dumped the tea and pulled out a flask of absinthe from my backpack. After filling up the now empty bottle, I tossed the flask into the warung's dustbin and tucked the bars of soap into my bag for safe-keeping. My goal: observe the jewellery store without arousing suspicion. I spotted an ATM security guard sitting out front; each shift was 12 hours long. Inside the store were two employees, a husband and wife. The owner was a man of Yemeni descent who'd turned 57 a couple of weeks earlier. I knew that because his birthday coincided with my first visit to the shop. He'd given me a piece of brownie and a date the size of my thumb. People call him Wan Ali.

I'd gone into the store to help a friend of mine pick out an engagement ring, but my plans changed when

Wan Ali showed me a black box the size of a cell phone. In a thick accent, he said, 'If you were the owner of this box, forget about asking for your in-laws' blessing—each of them would jump at the chance of marrying you.'

I recognized the box immediately.

'What about that one?' I pointed to a dull, violet-toned box painted with little flowers. It had been placed on a shelf alongside a few souvenirs from Mecca; in a photo above the box a teenage girl smiled sweetly. I'd redirected Wan Ali's focus so that he wouldn't think I'd taken an interest in the box he was holding.

'Oh, that was my late daughter's. There's nothing special about it.'

Wan Ali turned his attention to a broken electric fan that made a snapping sound every few seconds and leaked an oily liquid from its base. He apologized, wiping away grease with one hand while trying to secure the head of the fan with the other. The appliance stayed stable for barely a second. Realizing that it was a lost cause, he gave up and locked the black box in the display case and then took out a ring and started telling me about the gemstone.

The gemstone came from Planet Penus (he meant Venus). A chunk of red rock careened towards Earth and hit the Indian Ocean. Plummeting in temperature, a nearly transparent blue glaze appeared on the surface of the stone, leaving a berry-red dot the size of a pinhead at its core. If its owner is sinful, Wan Ali said, the ring will turn dark grey. While telling the story, he said the word *Penus ring* almost as often as the fan made its wounded squeal. I wondered, had he ever accidentally said the word *penis* to customers while bragging about the bauble he held in his hand?

I pestered him about the violet-toned box on the shelf. Again, he refused to show it to me, claiming it held nothing of value.

'Then show me what's inside the black box instead.'

He chuckled and chided me: it's forbidden to reveal secrets on a Friday. Changing the topic, he asked me why I had a dragon embroidered on my jacket. I was too dark-skinned to be Chinese, he said. I tersely replied, I'm not Chinese, but back in university I was in a lion-dance troupe. He believed me.

I had a feeling that I'd seen the black box before, but a hunch wasn't enough. I needed to see what lay inside. I tried to find out more about this Wan Ali fellow, and to learn how he'd got his hands on that box. I started visiting his jewellery store every day, subtly pumping his two employees for leads. Did I have anything better to do? Nah, I don't have a day job.

I began by questioning Nurida. She worked with Yadi, her husband, who held an IT degree from a mediocre university. Yadi, as the store's cashier, liked to greet customers with strange stories. His favourite conversation starter was, 'Have you heard about . . .'

When I prodded them about Wan Ali's personal life, Nurida and Yadi praised him effusively but failed to offer any concrete examples of their boss's many virtues. This, along with a half dozen other giveaways, made me confident they were lying. Maybe my sources were the problem. Good dogs wouldn't bite the hand that feeds them. Maimunah, Wan Ali's wife, on the other hand, was a more credible informant. Of Sundanese and Javanese descent, she was born and raised in the Kampung Melayu neighbourhood of Jakarta. Right away, she began blabbing about Wan Ali's depravity and didn't so much as pause when her husband walked within earshot. 'This sack of bones wants to get married again. Can you believe it? If he so much as tripped he'd be dead.' Wan Ali glared, angry. Yadi and Nurida giggled.

When I swung by the store the next day, I overheard an argument between the jeweller and his wife. Wan Ali, holding a chessboard under his left arm, seemed serious. He shook his head violently in disagreement, mouth agape and eyes bulging out of their sockets; he wagged his right index finger in Maimunah's face; he turned plum red, making his already unattractive features even uglier. I didn't want to see anyone get slapped, so I drew attention to myself by mimicking the satisfying pop of bubble gum by tapping my tongue against the roof of my mouth. I like to click out melodies when I'm not working. Even though clicking generally produces monotone sounds, I can imagine the different pitches in my head.

My click was particularly resonant. I may have achieved a new personal best for click volume. Wan Ali and Maimunah were shocked, like two thieves caught in the act. They stood there awkwardly until Wan Ali took the chessboard he'd been holding and said, 'Ah, there you are. How about a game of chess?' His body language, however, signalled he was not at all happy with my presence.

Despite my misanthropic tendencies, I can find ways to get a kick out of anyone. When it comes to chess, I'll be the first to admit that I have no special talent for the game and rarely come up with a clever move. That said, as far as I know, the knight always moves in an L shape, whether it's black or white or fucking turquoise. If there were an *Abridged Edition of Common Knowledge*, I'm pretty sure that rule would've been canonized in writing since mankind has come to a consensus on it. Maybe Wan Ali is the sole individual at odds with that consensus—or he's the only human being on the face of the planet who doesn't qualify as mankind, or quite the opposite, and he's the lone entity who represents all humanity. Who knows. All I can say for sure is that he picked up his knight and moved it five squares, in the shape of the letter S. He acted with total confidence, stroking his thin beard and not so much as glancing in my direction to gauge my reaction.

I moved my knight the way you're supposed to and captured his pawn as a rebuke: move your pieces like I do, like competitors do in any chess match I've ever seen, like every person who's ever played chess. It pushed him over the edge. Angrily, he accused me of being a stooge of Western liberal ideology.

'You know,' he said, jabbing his finger at me, 'infidels created an L-shaped move to sneak Liberal thought into the game. L clearly stands for Liberalism. It's a cheap trick—don't be so gullible.'

He corrected my knight's move and took back his pawn, warning me not to fall for a wolf in sheep's clothing. Me? I don't look anything like a sheep. I tapped my tongue against the roof of my mouth and thought about how insignificant I am in this universe, about all the things I don't know, and about how weird people can be. I came to the offhand conclusion that earth had been populated just to give me a few laughs.

From the moment I moved my knight until my opponent called checkmate, Wan Ali gabbed about his theory nonstop. I wanted to tell him that, in fact, the entire planet wholeheartedly believes in that conspiracy—each and every person, except for Wan Ali. That we're not just believers, but active participants—everyone, except for the man across from me. But I chose to keep mum, I didn't have the heart to hurt his feelings. I also refrained from teaching him the real rules of chess. I'm entertained by people who never grew out of naivety: innocent kids are adorable, and then as years pass, innocence starts to look a lot more like idiocy, which is no less amusing. I see no reason to correct stupid people; you might as well sit back and enjoy. Think of it as having a ticket to see lenong theatre or Rowan Atkinson playing Mr Bean.

The owner of the warung bugged me to take my change. Enough. I had 23 hours and 40-something minutes to wrangle together accomplices for a robbery. The plan was to steal the black box, but if they also felt like nabbing some gold or chopping up Wan Ali, so be it. My priority was taking a good look inside the box as soon as possible. I needed to come up with a plan, because if not, those 24 hours would pass me by. The simple thought of it raised my heartrate, not insignificantly.

Cortázar's engine rumbled. I started scheming about how to entice a certain English teacher into joining the heist. She was also an old high-school friend of mine, a former sepak takraw player, and my ex. We were very close, to the point that there isn't a thing I don't already know about her. Not so much her about me. Mentioning her full name would be too unwieldy for readers who hastily draw conclusions, so for your sake, I'll refer to her here as Kik. Earlier that day, I'd been reading a news article about the popularity of sepak takraw in Indonesia, and I couldn't help but think back to Kik's flexible body bending so she could whack the rattan ball with the inner curve of her foot. She was certainly skilled enough to battle Wan Ali.

I pulled the clutch towards me, switched gears and slowly released my grip while thinking about Kik.

*

Kik and I were together until a couple of months ago, when I'd gone over to her place and suggested she start dating Njet, my regular mechanic and a friend who designs steampunk weapons in his spare time. Njet is a committed Jehova's Witness who enjoys stories involving characters from the Gospel. My favourites are the zombie apocalypse variety. You know, the sort of thing where after the Great Flood recedes, all the people who drowned become zombies, and Admiral Noah fights tooth and nail to vanquish them. Njet's tales of the living dead—not to mention how a few viruses that turn men into walking corpses really exist—made us agree that there was no harm in building a few weapons for self-defence purposes. After all, every generation is convinced that it'll be the one to face the apocalypse. A guy like Njet would be a good match for Kik. The combination of engineering skills a la MacGyver and the lithe body of an athlete would produce offspring capable of winning an Olympic bronze in martial arts, at the very least. Kik was insulted. She smacked me, which was reasonable. She raised the topic of our unborn child and then said, if I really wanted to leave her, go ahead, leave. No need to fix her up with someone else. She announced that my words were very hurtful and that she would never forgive me. With a glare, she added that if she did get together with Njet after all, it'd be a choice she'd make on her own, with or without my advice. After sulking for a while longer, she fell silent. Maybe a new thought occurred to her, but she shut herself in her room without telling me what, so I left. By the time I got home, three voicemail notifications popped up on my screen. I set my phone on the counter and took a shower. My ringtone, the Boy Scout Hymn, played three or four more times. You should try it out, the feeling of lounging around in your underwear while hearing the Scout Hymn, pulling on a pair of dirty pants as the same song plays, trimming your fingernails in tune with the melody. It's a riot, the feeling that the Boy Scouts are guiding me, supervising my every move from dawn till dusk.

At approximately 11 p.m., I returned Kik's calls and stated that my decision to become a detective was final. Being a private eye was a profession full of hardship and danger, and I didn't want to put another person's life at risk. Kik had demanded an explanation for my behaviour, and that's the excuse I sputtered out, spying on a pile of *The Three Investigators* books on a nearby table. But no reason would ever be enough for Kik: one justification produced a new question, which in turn led to more demands, and so on. This business of breaking up was a matter of who'd get bored first. Would I get tired of talking or would she, listening? We were at an impasse: I love banter, and as far I as I can remember, Kik's never taken issue with being on the receiving end of drivel. Flipping through the titles of the children's detective stories, I improvised a list of dangers that could befall a detective, each accompanied by compelling reasons why Kik was particularly ill suited to accompany me in my investigations:

1. Have you heard of the 'Terror Castle'? A detective can't refuse to go inside. And you're scared of haunted houses, aren't you?

2. What about the case of the 'Whispering Mummy'? If you're a detective, you can't attack someone when they speak in hushed tones. Oh, come on, don't you remember the time you kicked that parking attendant in the balls when he mumbled obscene comments about you under his breath?

3. You never know, I might have to solve a case like *The Mystery of the Screaming Clock*. Good detectives aren't meant to run when they hear sudden, loud noises, and you always dash into the kitchen when the kettle starts boiling, don't you?

4. Think about how risky it is to deal with dangerous animals, like in the case of the 'Nervous Lion'. Okay, okay, you're right, it's me who hates cats. I'm not planning on becoming a cat-lover just to investigate some stressed-out Simba, but still, I don't want you to end up being his lunch. A lion is a lion, no matter how nervous.

5. Now, there also are investigations in which a detective has to be brave enough to spoon-feed medicine to a 'Coughing Dragon'. Bear with me—picture this creature's ability to burn you to a crisp. Next, imagine someone with a cough, often a symptom of a head cold. If that dragon sneezes, what's coming out of its nostrils?

I kept listing any possible risk I could come up with until Kik was fed up. She raised all sorts of irrelevant details, reminding me that I was 35 years old, unemployed and a failed writer. Finally, she demanded I explain why I'd told her to start dating Njet. I had no particular reason in mind, so rather than invent yet another excuse, I offered a rendition of the theme song to the cartoon *Nobody's Boy: Remi* in tongue flaps. She hung up. In the weeks following the breakup, I put some thought into looking for a job. I need to work if I want to seem normal, I told Cortázar. Soon enough, Cortázar would lead me to Wan Ali, and Wan Ali would lead me to the black box. You could say it was all a coincidence, but for me, this is the story of how I found my life's calling: it was the moment I became a private eye.

*

Cortázar and I wove between five or six cars. At the stoplight, we rolled to a halt next to an old yellow Datsun. I glanced through the open window and saw a group of teenagers, probably skipping school. The driver's hand was lolling out the open window; his pinched face and bushy moustache, far too thick for someone of his age, reminded me of a weasel's. I met his gaze while channelling thoughts about the consequences of cutting class. He returned my look with an icy stare and flicked his cigarette. I could only make out the torso of the boy in the passenger seat, he was clutching a can of San Miguel. If

29

the kid wasn't just a loser, he probably suffered from acute melancholy. In 10 years, he'll jump straight into a tiger pit, San Miguel in hand. A girl sat alone in the back-seat, frowning and rubbing at her face as though she found the very existence of her eyes, nose, and mouth disturbing. I could offer my assistance. It's not so difficult to smooth something down with a bit of sandpaper and woodchips. The depressing atmosphere was stifling, so much so that I was tempted to light some hot peppers on fire and toss them into the back of the car to brighten the mood. Soon enough, the car lurched forward, but it was no use: from a simple glance you could tell those kids weren't going anywhere.

Cortázar started overheating right as we hit a traffic jam. I had to rev his engine, switch gears, then twist his brake lever every few seconds; rev his engine, brake again. Poor Cortázar. I glanced at my watch. Kik would only be out of class at 3 p.m., which meant I had an hour to grab a drink and a smoke and give my motorbike a rest. I decided to stop at the nearest bar.

An event of some sort was taking place inside. Someone was lecturing and a dozen or so teenagers gathered around to listen. Ten servers milled about, taking orders. The speaker was analysing *Fight Club* through a Nietzschean lens with an intensity that made it seem as though this was the only movie to have ever been created. Why *Fight Club*? Why not *The Turin Horse*? Admittedly, *Fight Club* made a bigger splash in pop culture. The group started debating nihilism with a degree of brutality that rivalled *A Clockwork Orange*. Marla's name was mentioned on multiple occasions; they must've found her character very compelling. Unfortunately, I had no reason to offer my two cents. Nihilism will always sell, with me or without me. I half-heartedly paid attention for the free beer.

A girl sitting near me, in her early twenties, I'd guess, appeared solemnly engaged in the event despite acoustics that made the speaker's voice bounce off the walls like a priest's in a cathedral. She was wearing a maroon knit cardigan over a white t-shirt. I could smell her perfume, the kind that tried to say, 'I'm a smart, good girl.' You know, a scent that's not too strong but just sharp enough to tickle your nose. I sneezed. She turned to look at me, smiled with an awkward nod, and then resumed her earlier posture.

'. . . 15 years ago, Budi Alazon wore that red mask to Slank concerts when they were on tour for the album Suit-Suit . . . He he. Honestly, that mask was way better,' a guy sitting behind me gabbed. 'It's classic. But maybe he felt the need to rebrand his "colour" to stay relevant.'

'But fucking hell, why *pink*?' asked a guy with a thick Batak accent. Glasses clinked. 'Looks like a pig's ass. Not macho at all.'

'Hey, people say he chose pink to get sponsored by a tampon company. Look it up.'

'*Martole*. That's bullshit. As a dedicated fan since elementary school, I'm pissed.'

'He doesn't even do shows anymore, you know. Makes it all seem a bit fake, like he's strapped for cash. He disappears for 15 years and all of sudden, he's back? I thought he died.'

'What son of a bitch doesn't need money these days? And you're not the only one who thought he was dead. *Rolling Stone Indonesia* did a special edition on the Budi Alazon investigation, remember? There were five theories: drowning, deadly fever, AIDS, kidnapped by Suharto's minions, poison. His name recognition boomed after the scandal, and even I started believing that something crazy must've happened. Get famous and then suddenly vanish? Sounds like a pretty sick way to become a legend to me. But yeah, it's probably the money. You know how much a ticket to the Dewa 19 reunion concert cost? Enough to buy a hundred cases of cigarettes—and those tickets sold out. Sold. Out. People have a thing for nostalgia, anything from Budi Alazon to Ahmad Dhani.'

'Hey, Ringworm, don't mention Ahmad Dhani and Budi Alazon in the same sentence. They're not on the same level. We're talking about a god here, not some poser.'

Someone shifted in their seat.

'Whatever. Back to the question: why pink?'

'Maybe it's some reference to, I dunno, a feminist campaign or an LGBTQ movement.'

'Are you saying he's gay?'

'We can't even be sure he's a guy. Have you ever seen him without that mask on?'

'Nah, with a voice like his there's no way he's a girl. And the tattoo, remember? Supposedly it represents the battle cry of a man-eating bird.'

'Like I said, he's a god. And as long as he wears that mask, we won't know if he's human or ghost.'

'Yeah, yeah. You're right. He's . . . a god. God doesn't need gender.'

'Did you get your ticket?'

I wondered—if God ever came down to Earth, would mankind be disappointed?

The girl next to me stood up, glancing at me. She shook off her cardigan as she walked by, tying it around her waist. Only then did I notice that her shirt had an image of Budi Alazon on it, the rock star that the boys behind me were complaining about. Under the image were the words *Gelora Bung Karno Stadium* printed in an old western font, and beneath that, the date of the concert, which would take place the next day. From the chit-chat I'd overheard—which sounded more like trash-talking than a proper conversation—I gathered that doors would open at noon, even though the rockstar wouldn't go on stage until 4 p.m. Maybe it really would be packed. Someone in the group, the guy with the Batak accent, called for the bill.

The girl still hadn't returned to her table. Two guys from the group behind me had also left. I was curious about the Batak one. I've only ever known three Batak people: the first was Marina Alfi Siregar, my stepmother, a very wise woman. We'd split my father's inheritance down the middle. Once we parted ways, she opened a restaurant with her cut of the money; I'd turned my garage into a reading room. It wasn't successful in the least, so I converted it into a recording studio and gambled off the rest. All that remained of my late father was a dilapidated colonial-style house begging to be taken out of its misery. That, and Cortázar. The second Batak person in my life is an expert tire repairman I call Lae, to whom I entrust Cortázar. To this day, I don't know a thing about his family. The third Batak—though in this case I'm not entirely sure of his heritage—is Artur Harahap, a novelist and short-story writer from the '70s. His work taught me what it means to craft a good story: all I did was change some punctuation, fix the typos, adjust the outdated terms, and replace his name with mine. The story won a creative-writing competition four years ago and was reprinted in an anthology of contest winners from the past decade. If you ever happen upon the book *Our Engine Is Very Loud and That Changes Nothing*, look for the contribution with the same title—that's it, Harahap's creation. I still get raging heartburn every time I remember how an internationally acclaimed novelist deemed the story 'original'. A different writer commented that the prose was 'innovative and fresh', and didn't hesitate before adding, 'a new literary brother is in our midst'. Unbelievable, right? You reap what you sow. Beats me what they were blathering on about, I was in it for the money. Ten million rupiah in cash. Enough to give Cortázar a paint job and blow the rest gambling. If only the commemorative plaque were worth something, I could've put it down as a bet . . .

I went out to the parking lot and saw the girl with the rock star t-shirt pointing a broken beer bottle at two guys cornered against a motorbike. At first, I thought she was defending herself against the hulking men. Maybe they'd tried to harass her. I realized I was wrong when she yelled, 'Hand it over. Now!' Her victims seemed unimpressed.

I lit a cigarette and sauntered over to the group, placing my left hand in my pocket and arranging my fingers to make it look like I had a pistol. I asked what was going on in an exaggerated, tough-guy tone. Classic trick.

'This crazy chick wants a Budi Alazon ticket,' the guy on the left said.

'So give it to her,' I replied, pointing my left hand in his direction. 'Or I'll make that beer you just drank leave your body, and not through your mouth.'

'B-but I didn't drink beer, bro.'

'Yeah, he just ordered a juice.'

'In that case, you're not gonna be able to tell the difference between what's blood and what's juice.' I moved my hand threateningly, raising and lowering my index finger to mix things up, and got a bit more in their face. 'Hey, you,' I said to the one on the right. 'Are you really about to trade your friend's life for a concert ticket?'

Suddenly, a blow landed somewhere between my Adam's apple and chin. I could feel the impact reverberate from my jaw to my ears and through my skull. My limbs wouldn't budge, but I heard a motorbike speed away in a cloud of exclamations in Batak and two-stroke exhaust.

Next thing I knew, I felt something cold. Then, I heard a sigh, followed by a voice that reverberated as though it were emerging from the mouth of a cave: 'He got you with his left hook.'

A bottle of cold beer was being held to my head. The girl repeated herself, adding, '. . . if he'd used his right hand, you'd be dead. But instead, you're still here, making my life difficult.'

The bottle left my forehead. The girl popped the cap and set it down on the pavement next to me.

Blinking, I tried to wrap my head around what happened: I'm lying in a parking lot. Some guy clocked me, and I lost consciousness. Punched, passed out in a parking lot—and then, the girl I'd been trying to help stayed to take care of me. That girl, the one helping me, is handing me a bottle of beer.

A chilled beverage might hit the spot. The cold sensation would remind me of the boy whose frozen corpse gets ravaged by dogs in Hemingway's *The Snows of*

Kilimanjaro. The character comforts me; for some reason, he makes me think of Jakarta. Whenever I think about Hemingway, Agnes von Kurowsky immediately comes to mind. That's why, if I meet someone new in the city and don't feel like putting in any effort, I'll call them Hemingway if they're a guy and Agnes if they're a girl.

'I could've killed them if I'd wanted to, you know.' I sat up and took a big swig of beer.

'With this?' She made the shape of a pistol with her right hand.

'No. With this,' I pointed my left index finger like I wanted to shoot, then clicked my tongue against the roof of my mouth.

She laughed. 'Whatever you say, Mr Eastwood.'

'Wow. You're the type who watches *Fight Club* at least three times a day, aren't you?'

'I've never seen it,' she replied. 'Which probably makes you wonder, why would I show up at an event about a movie I've never seen? Well, here's my answer: I came here to take what's rightfully mine. Those guys who punched you stole my concert ticket. Maybe "steal" is the wrong word, but I stood behind one of them in line and then he bought the last two tickets. Two tickets, but only one person waiting! That's fucking rude, I'd been on my feet for over two hours and some person who didn't even show up practically plucks the ticket from my fingers. No fucking respect!'

'What a heart-warming story. But I wouldn't have asked you about that in the first place. Here's what I want to know: how do you feel about adrenaline?'

Instead of answering, the girl pointed at her shirt, indicating that all she wanted was to go to the concert.

'You know, you can watch Woodstock '69 without all the trouble of time travel. That's why they made YouTube.'

'There's nothing like seeing your idol in person.'

I cleared my throat and muttered, 'Bullshit.'

She leaned away from me with a glare and an accusation. 'You must be a Taurus.'

'I actually decided to switch to Scorpio last year. Why?'

'Everyone who annoys the hell out of me is a Taurus.'

'Suharto's face annoys me, and he was a Gemini. But gremlins, are they any less irksome, what with their pesky habit of chucking gravel at pilots? I bet they don't have astrological signs. How about speed bumps? Or an umbrella that gets stuck when you open it? Or a broken zipper? All annoying, no astrology involved.'

'I like you better when you're knocked out. Seriously, you're much sweeter.'

I looked down at my watch. 3.18 p.m.

'I'm cutting it close. If you're curious, walk with me to my motorbike and sit down behind me. No chit-chat. And remember one thing: don't touch me, especially not from behind.'

I walked briskly towards Cortázar without checking to see if the girl planned to join me. She was waiting to my left by the time I put on my helmet, and before I had a chance to secure the strap, she'd swiped it off my head and set it on her own. Irritating, but I didn't say anything. I scooted forward so she could mount Cortázar, and she settled on his rump without a word. Just as we'd agreed.

It's illegal to ride without a helmet, so I avoided the bigger streets. It was nearly evening: dusk drew over the sky and commuters, worn out even though it was the beginning of the month, were about to start flooding the highways as they headed home from work. If I were a policeman, this would be the perfect time to line my pockets with some extra cash.

'Hey, Agnes,' I said, glancing over my shoulder. I had to repeat myself four times before the passenger riding behind me deigned to answer. 'I hope you're familiar with this area, because I have no clue how to get out of here without getting pulled over.'

'My name isn't Agnes. But yeah, I've been here before. Turn left up ahead,' she said. We turned right. 'What's the plan, are we going to kill someone?'

'Don't pretend you know what we're about to do.'

'What could possibly pump you with more adrenaline than taking someone's life?'

'A lot of things,' I retorted. 'Biting off the end of a firecracker and lighting the wick, for one.'

'No way you have the balls.'

'Says who? I could beat you back and blue with the soles of my shoes, then deposit you by the banks of the canal over there. Hm, or maybe I'd tie a rope around your wrist, secure the other end to Cortázar's handlebar, and drag you there. The entire time you'd be bouncing across the asphalt. You'd lose one of your ears, your nose, and one of your breasts at the least. You'd be screaming for mercy, and I'd just murmur *no one can help you now.*'

'If you say so. But you don't have the guts. You're a loser. The way you talk shows exactly how scared you are. I knew it the second you opened your mouth.'

'Hey, my shoes are real leather. You could rub out a cigarette on them.'

'Sitting here listening to this bullshit makes me more and more convinced that you're all talk, no action.'

'Now you're just lying, it's so obvious. If I'm as lame as you say, what would make you want to tag along?'

'I wanted to start a list: Things That Give You an Adrenaline Rush—Loser Edition.'

'We're committing a robbery. Tomorrow.'

'Who are we planning on stealing from? An elementary schooler, a pregnant woman, an old man who can barely walk, or some ramshackle warung by the side of the road?'

'Not quite. It'll be a bit more challenging than that.'

'What, then?' she asked, but without giving me time to answer, she continued. 'Tie a rope to the warung and drag it around with this old motorbike? Is that the plan?'

'This is Cortázar, Agnes. Not any old motorbike. He has free will and has practised holding his temper since before you were born.'

'A motorbike is a motorbike.'

'Do I need to hop off right now and let Cortázar carry you wherever he pleases?'

'Go ahead, if you think you have it in you.'

I liked this Agnes girl, even though I didn't know her real name. Her argumentative spirit reminded me of own when I was in my mid-twenties. I love reminiscing on those days; what comes to mind is the half-built Tower of Babel before God came and smashed it to the ground.

'So, why do you go by Agnes?' I inquired.

'I should be the one asking you that. What made that name come to mind when you met me?'

'Who said anything about when I met you . . .'

'Just a guess. Was Agnes an ex-girlfriend?'

'Stop acting like you know me. When other people do that, I hit them over the head with a brick.'

She sighed noisily, raising goosebumps on the nape of my neck. 'Is that so? In that case, I'll opt for the brick.'

'It'd be my pleasure, Agnes, but it's not appropriate to crack skulls in this neighbourhood.'

'My name's Afif. I think it's best you get it through your head that I'd rather be knocked out than hear you call me Agnes again. Turn left up ahead.' But Cortázar turned right. From her next intake of breath, I could tell that she was getting tired of arguing. 'All right then, what are we going to rob?'

'A jewellery store.'

*

A few metres before the next intersection, I spotted an elderly woman on the pavement cradling a small cardboard box. She looked to her left and right. I pulled over nearby and asked what on earth she was doing standing by the road at dusk. She told me that her bathroom light had gone out and that she was waiting for her husband to come home and replace the bulb. Afif grumbled when I offered to help. Earlier I'd said, 'We're close,' and now she could hardly wait to rob the store. I explained that there were some 19 and a half hours remaining before the robbery and, not to worry, the people we needed to wrangle together didn't have the spare cash to skip town. But kids these days have no patience. 'You have to learn the art of waiting,' I told Afif. 'And the art of plotting.'

'It's not like anyone waits for the perfect time to die. You could die at any moment, so there's no point in fussing over plans,' she replied. 'Surely you understand that if something as important as death can come unexpectedly, there's no point in delaying a robbery.'

I liked the way she always said, 'if you say so' or 'surely you understand'. Surely she'd understand how those expressions carry an air of impertinence that makes it fitting to call her a modern Agnes von Kurowsky. 'But then you'd be dying at the right time,' I replied. 'Which means the plan for your life was carried out after all.'

The old woman admonished me. 'Are you still going to help?' she asked. I gave her a thumbs-up and smiled. That's how people typically say yes. I slid off Cortázar and started making small talk.

As we approached the woman's house, we were greeted by a Toyota Starlet, a 1994 or 1996 model. A large birdcage resembling a krepuk tin was hanging by the side of the garage. The house could've been nice if someone younger had been in charge of upkeep. The choice of white wall paint made the objects in each room stand out: the natural wood cabinets and dining table, the blue sofa for receiving guests, the red plastic cups, the dried banana peel lying on the table, which spoke to the resident's messy habits. The house didn't smell, probably because little dishes of ground coffee were placed in every corner, even in the bathroom, where I spotted at least four. I went over to one and noted that the grounds were fresh. While changing the lightbulb, I wondered what kind of old person would regularly restock all this coffee but neglect to throw away a banana peel. Afif picked up on the strange atmosphere and whispered that something was off about the old woman. She'd seen a row of jam jars filled with cloudy water and holding dead Siamese fighting fish. I tried to calm her down: 'Just because the old lady collects fish corpses doesn't mean she's crazy.' I myself wasn't convinced.

When we sat down in the living room to enjoy a snack, I asked the woman one simple question—'Who else lives with you?'—and she replied with a lengthy story. The sofa would've been roomy enough for three were it not for a large crate with straw sticking through the slats on one cushion, which forced me and Afif to sit right next to each other. Our knees and elbows kept bumping every now and again, and if either of us moved, the other was sure to be jostled. Afif was doing most of the nudging. She also stepped on my shoe twice, in an effort to signal that she was getting tired of this woman's babble. It didn't bother me.

The old woman, Tati S. Abdillah by name, was 80. She and her husband, Bachtiar S. Abdillah, had lived in this housing complex ever since their only child, Suryadi S. Abdillah, had turned five. He was now 35 and married. Tati opened a photo album. Every time she pointed at a photo she'd tell us a story, and it went on like that until we arrived at a picture of Bachtiar and a man who appeared to be of Arab descent, whose arms were around each other's shoulders. I'd have guessed they were under 50 when the photo was taken. Bachtiar was giving a thumbs up and the man by his side had a black box tucked under his arm. Tati proclaimed the man's full name: Ali bin Usam bin Yasser al-Kindi. I prefer to call him Wan Ali.

'This man,' Tati said, 'married an old maid named Maimunah. They had a daughter, whom he married off to a lecherous old man. Maimunah is my sister. We were nine in total. I'm the eldest, and Maimunah is the eighth. The second, fourth and fifth all died of smallpox. The third was stillborn, the seventh disappeared after inheriting my father's export business, never to be heard from again. The ninth died of kidney failure at an early age from consuming too many energy drinks. You could say that Maimunah is the only family I have left, but we're not close. She thinks I wronged her because I didn't support her marriage. Personally, I have no idea how she fell for that scrawny Arab. He's wealthy, I'll give him that, but everyone knows that he owes his success to whatever's inside that black box he's holding in the photo.'

Afif snorted. She seemed like the sort who'd be sceptical of mysticism. She whispered in my ear, 'When can we finish with this bullshit and start planning the heist?'

I told her to hold tight just a bit longer.

'What's inside the box?'

Afif kicked at my feet, but I didn't feel anything.

'There are countless rumours, but I only believe one: that it contains a strand of Uwais al-Qarni's hair.'

'Who's that?' Afif whispered.

'No clue. Might be a poet, given the name,' I muttered in response. 'Or a long-lost relative of Iko Uwais. You know, the martial arts expert.'

'He studied under the Prophet,' Tati clarified, as though she'd overheard what we'd been whispering about. 'He wasn't famous here on Earth, but he is known in heaven for his devotion to his mother.'

'I'm not actually so tight with Muhammad, but his reputation precedes him. Word is he was a very good person,' I propped my chin on my hand, preparing to listen to a lengthy story. Tati's gaze took on the intensity of a cat studying a ball of yarn.

Tati meticulously described what Uwais looked like: blue eyes, red hair, broad-chested, strapping, and tall, quick to smile, etc. She talked about his good deeds, his admirable qualities, his this and his that, but she never got around to explaining how a piece of old hair could make someone rich. I told her that I enjoyed listening to her stories, and I wasn't lying. I was impressed by the expression that came over her face as she dredged up tales about Uwais: her eyelids fluttered, her brow furrowed, and the wrinkles that dashed across her cheeks as she selected words to describe a man so venerated by the greatest religion in the world reminded me of the cresting waves that surfers love. Her word choice was so cautious that each sentence she uttered was a cliché. Her nose seemed to struggle with every intake of breath, as though she had just summitted Mount Everest. It got to the point where I'd gasp along with her, in fear of losing my share of oxygen. After three or four long breaths, she reached her conclusion, 'And those are the virtues of Uwais al-Qarni.'

I heard a different kind of noisy exhale from the individual at my side, one that I'd loosely translate as: 'Are we done yet?'

Then, with my own sigh, I tried to communicate: 'But how does any of this relate to a magic snippet of hair?'

I stared at Tati, Tati stared at Afif, Afif stared at me. A Mexican standoff with pupils instead of pistols. Unable to stand the awkwardness, Afif drew out one of her cigarettes. Seeing this, Tati grabbed Afif's pack and shook out one for herself, licking the filter. I followed suit and tucked one between my lips. I could only think of two ways to break the ice in such a situation. 'What an incredible story,' I said, opting for the second method. Trust me, no one would have appreciated my choosing the first. 'But Tati, your husband still hasn't come home.'

'That's the problem. He's been gone since last night. I'm quite worried . . .' Tati rubbed her face, bringing out the wrinkles and adding another 10 years to her age. 'Bachtiar started acting strange when we got a computer,' she continued, pointing to the adjacent room. A desktop monitor stood on a table next to a sewing machine. 'He never used to laze around at home all day. On the contrary, he could hardly keep still. He was always wetting down the street, tending to the garden, things like that. But ever since Yadi bought him that computer, all he wants to do is sit in front of the screen. He's online all day and even forgets to eat.'

'On Facebook?' Afif guessed.

'Yes. Just like a teenager. Last night as he left, he told me he was going to meet an old friend. From high school, maybe. I'm sure they connected through social media.'

'Do you know if your husband's friend has a profile too?' Afif asked.

Tati shook her head. 'It must be her kids. I bet they recognized Bachtiar in a photo and talked to their mother about him. Ever since, the two have been chatting on the phone. My husband calls her all the time. I swear I don't object, it's just . . .'

'Jealousy?' Afif queried.

Tati shook her head once more. 'No, I don't feel jealous. I'm annoyed, that's all.'

'It's getting late. Is your husband's memory at all faulty?' I saw Afif lift her leg and squash my shoe. Again, I felt nothing.

'No, no. He should be home any minute now.'

'Yes, of course.' I took a kastengel from the jar on the table and chewed it thoughtfully. 'If I were your husband, I'd definitely come home. There's no way his high-school friend can be as pretty as you.'

I'm not one for false compliments. Almost everything I said was true. Tati looked neither pretty nor ugly with her wrinkles. What I mean is, the vast majority of Indonesians, as they reach the age in which they slowly crawl towards death– 60 or 70 years old—develop the kind of wrinkles that are basically impossible to conceal. Anyone that age has no choice but to accept the webs of lines on their skin; everyone else, meanwhile, should be careful to select kind words to address them. Only a real jerk would hurt the feelings of someone so old. In other words, when someone approaches 70, the terms *pretty* and *ugly* hold very little weight. The compliment I gave was honest, if meaningless.

Tati smiled, and when she did, she looked two years younger. I pulled the iced-tea bottle from my backpack and took a sip. The room felt brighter. 'We should probably get going.'

'Oh, one more thing,' Tati stopped us at the door. I hoped she wasn't planning on asking us to watch the DVD on the coffee table, *The Collapse of Darwin's Theory.* I brainstormed three excuses to refuse such an invitation without hurting her feelings. For example: I could explain that I'd rather she stab a straw into my ear and slurp out my own brain slush like coconut water than watch a film directed by Adnan Oktar. As though she'd read my mind, Tati left the DVD untouched and instead opened the protective plastic from the page of the album. Removing the most recent photo of Bachtiar, she handed it to Afif, whose arms were crossed tightly over her chest. I was starting to think that my young friend should've popped a Valium a few hours before we'd met, that's how paranoid she was acting. It wasn't the first time I'd seen her so stiff, standing like she were afraid her organs would leap from her body and flee.

'I'm not sure about what I said before. Maybe my husband did get lost. He's not so young any more, after all. Will you help me look for him?' she asked. I noticed the album page held a few copies of the same photo. It seemed that Tati made a habit of bestowing pictures of Bachtiar upon her guests. I agreed to help. Afif kicked my shoe one last time and still I felt nothing.

'All right, we're off. If there are any developments from us regarding Bachtiar, we'll be in touch right away.' I slipped my foot back into the empty shoe Afif had been abusing.

'You weren't wearing your shoes that whole time?'

I grinned sheepishly.

'That's not funny, you know.'

'Oh, I know. It's the kind of joke that hasn't been funny since the eighties. But stepping on someone's foot to express discontent is also pretty passé.'

'Right, and now you're an expert on slapstick.'

I took the photo of Bachtiar from Afif and slid it into my back pocket. We said goodbye. Tati and Afif shook hands for so long that I felt like a TV camera capturing a heart-warming scene, a mother–daughter pair reuniting after a 20-year separation.

'What, were you trying to avoid kissing those wrinkly cheeks?' I asked once we'd passed through the front door.

Afif sniffed the air near the birdcage in lieu of a reply. 'It doesn't smell like anything's in here.'

'Maybe the fowl flew the coop.'

She stood on tiptoes to get a better look and shook her head. 'I told you, there's something wrong with that woman.'

I craned my neck and spotted a scattering of bones and a single dull purple marble. 'You're quick to judge,' I said. 'A lot of people collect animal bones as a hobby. That, or Tati has taken an interest in archaeology.'

She walked away from me. I followed. When we reached Cortázar, I handed her my helmet.

'Put it on,' I said.

'You're not the boss of *aing*!'

'If you're Sundanese, you must know that *aing* is a very rude way to refer to yourself.'

'I'm not Sundanese.'

'And I'm not wrong.'

Afif shifted her weight, making Cortázar sway from side to side. 'About what? *Aing* is rude, sure. But Sundanese? A few words in Zulu wouldn't make me South African.'

I fired up the engine and made a U-turn. Afif shouted in my ear to ask why we were going that way, even though we were moving so slowly that she had no need to raise her voice.

'It's not up to me. Cortázar chooses the route.'

'Stop saying this hunk of metal is sentient,' she said. 'You're driving me crazy.'

We were meant to go straight at the next intersection but made a left instead.

'This is the exact street we drove down before. Don't tell me you're trying to take me back to that bar filled with adolescent Brad Pitt fans.'

There I was again, desperate to articulate that this was out of my control, but if I'd repeated myself, chances are she'd have jumped off the motorbike, hit the pavement and ended up with a concussion. I didn't have time to take her to the hospital. So, while clicking my tongue like a ticking clock, I moved the conversation in a different direction: 'We're going to look for Bachtiar. I happen to be acquainted with someone who definitely knows him.'

'Who?'

'His son.'

—TRANSCRIPT II—

You called the vegetable market, and the individual who picked was a certain Bambang Trimutri, correct?

Which part?

Did you dial the market?

Yes.

And the person who answered, was he a man with a deep voice, Bambang Trimutri?

He had a deep voice, yes, but I don't know a Bambang Trimutri.

Bambang Trimutri owns the market.

Oh, really? Sounds like a politician's name.

Bambang asked an employee to drop the corn off at your house at approximately 5.30 p.m. Indonesian Standard Time. Did you receive the delivery?

Wow. Sir, it seems you know more than I do. I'm starting to understand why you'd become a police detective. I was doubtful, but now I see that you're actually very perceptive. You even know things that I haven't told you. You remind me of that famous detective from Sukabumi. What was his name? Oh, right, Poirot.

Poirot isn't from Sukabumi. And it's pronounced *pwa-row*.

Really? Sounds to me like a Sukabumi kind of name.

Moving on. What did you do when you received the delivery?

I whipped up a batch of porridge, just for Jenifer. I have a secret recipe, one that my husband and I came up with to make Jenifer sing sweetly. A long time ago we had our parrot Rudi convert to Islam. After eating our porridge day after day, Rudi learned to mimic our recitation of both lines of the Shahada. And all we did was mix date juice and Zamzam water into the corn! Oops, I just gave away the ingredients. But I suppose it's not such a big deal, since you're a policeman. I'm not sure if your profession requires any oaths on keeping secrets, but detectives must have some talent at discretion, at least in theory.

So, you got the corn and prepared the bird feed. What next?

I fed her. Jenifer won't eat if she isn't hand-fed. My my, is that bird spoiled. She even has her own spoon. The thing is, Jenifer receives special treatment that none of our other pets ever got. Like that spoon I mentioned. And her bathwater has to be filtered. We don't want her to get a parasite. We also spruced up her cage with a purple marble. I bought it at the market downtown when our daughter-in-law was close to giving birth. We'd only planned on buying strollers and baby clothes, but I started looking at other things, you know how mothers are. Jenifer seemed so happy with that marble. She stands on top of it when she thinks no one's looking. I like to sit on the couch and peek at her through the window. Typical daughter, so shy. I always wanted a little girl of my own, but what can you do? We can't choose the sex of our children.

And then, after feeding Jenifer?

Hold on. Do you think feeding her's easy? She goes on hunger strikes. The first time, I was so confused I almost cried. Then I thought about my son, back when he was little. I used to sing him a lullaby I made up, to calm him down when he cried.

> *My love for you*
> *stretches from the earth to the moon*
> *from the moon to Medan*
> *and on to Honolulu*

I forget how the rest goes, so I sang that verse to myself again and again until I felt tired. When I stopped, Jenifer hopped towards me. Incredible, right? I was so overjoyed I almost ate her porridge myself. Then I fed her while I hummed the tune. I did that for around a week until I started feeling sad for some reason. Maybe because I didn't have the strength to keep singing, my voice has grown weaker as I've aged. Finally, I decided to go to the market and buy a cassette of children's music. But the weird thing is, no one sells cassettes any more. They suggested I buy a CD player. Fine. I bought one along with some CDs of children's music and played them for Jenifer. That only worked for a few days, though, and when the bird realized she'd been fooled, she resumed her hunger strike. Jenifer's smart. Sometimes I think she can read my mind.

Then . . . after feeding Jenifer?

I taught her how to count, 1 to 10. Sometimes I read her short stories from the newspaper. But I haven't lately, the stories don't make very much sense these days. In medicine, we're taught to have expertise on each organ before carrying out an experiment, say, grafting a monkey head onto a bear cub body, for example. Fiction nowadays skips the basics. I'm no writer, but you don't need to be one yourself to see when something isn't done correctly. Oh, and Jenifer's interested in politics and international affairs. She and I listen to Radio Republik Indonesia on the veranda for hours. Maybe that's what I did that morning, three days ago. I listen to the radio every day without fail, sometimes in the morning, sometimes in the afternoon or evening. In other words, if I didn't listen that morning, I definitely would've tuned in later in the day.

Was there a witness to any of this?

Of course. God.

Anyone besides God?

There is no God but Allah, sir.

No, what I'm asking is, can any human being confirm your account of what you were doing the morning in question? A neighbour, for example.

My neighbour is a man of Indian descent. We call him Sir Shakur. He is so very considerate. You could always count on him to hire a fogging service for our block, which meant that when other neighbourhoods were hit hard by dengue, we were spared.

Before he became rich, Sir Shakur was an orphan who worked peeling potatoes at a market near the docks. He'd gut fish, haul sacks of rice, deliver groceries. As a teenager, he spent his free time at the junkyard. That's where he found a black box that would make him prosper.

Sir Shakur has a child, a son who's as decent a man as he. The son has a personal assistant who is also kind, not to mention pretty. Sir Shakur would send this assistant to my house each week to bring me kue kering. Very delicious. By then his son already lived outside the city, organizing the family business. I know all about Sir Shakur and his son's assistant. Oh, and the assistant is still single, you know. Are you married? If not, I'd be happy to introduce the two of you.

I'd rather we continue. Did Sir Shakur pay you a visit that morning?

Of course not, I'd run away if I saw him. He died 30 years ago. He left that black box to his son in his will. But his son doesn't believe in mystical nonsense, so he gave the box to my husband. I didn't like that he accepted the gift, and in protest I refused to speak to him while the object was in his possession. Finally, he offered the box to my brother-in-law. My husband, my brother-in-law and Sir Shakur's son were in business together. 'When one of us prospers, so do we all.' That's what my husband used to say.

I couldn't care less about this box. Stick to the point. Who can confirm that you were feeding your bird that morning? And where's your husband?

Oh my, there you go again, cutting me off. Please don't. I'll have to start over from the beginning.

[The witness repeats her account of the morning.]

—END OF AUDIO FILE—

CHEETAH JINNI

Knit skull cap

Kalimaya opal

Hematite

Gold
thread

Amethyst

Smoky
quartz

Sumatran
jade

Tiger's
eye quartz

Polyester
sarong

Chiffon
shoulder
cloth

In the early 1980s, the Cheetah Jinni was brought to Indonesia as an exotic
pet and sold to the family of the wealthiest man in West Java, Pak Sumarjo.
Contained to an empty field, surrounded by an iron fence, the Cheetah Jinni
missed being able to hunt, to sprint after his prey. He grew frustrated and
one day hurled himself towards the fence at full speed.

03

I'm going to rob the jewellery store, and Cortázar and Afif are in on the plan. Eighteen hours left on the clock.

I used to be crazy about Spike, the green stegosaurus from *The Land before Time*. Suryadi S. Abdillah—aka Yad—reminded me of Spike with his pot-belly, protruding chin and droopy eyes. I wouldn't be surprised if it turned out he had a humpback. But it wouldn't make sense to nickname Yadi Spike. The alias was too cool for him. Better to call him Pongo instead.

When we entered the store, Yadi was sitting at the cash register, daydreaming. He had that blank look on his face that people get when they don't need to imagine the future, since what they did yesterday, and again today, looks exactly like what they'll do tomorrow. I was tempted to lob a grenade at him, if only I had one. I could hear the ticking. Lately, Yadi's been making that tsk sound whenever he sees me, maybe because of the offer I made him the other day.

'You can forget about it,' he said. 'I haven't changed my mind.'

'Oh, but you will.' I sat down next to him and threw my arm over his shoulder. 'Pongo, meet Agnes. Agnes, Pongo.'

Yadi furrowed his brow as though about to ask, *what do you mean, Pongo?* but he looked as though he didn't have it in him to correct his own name.

Afif stretched out her hand and introduced herself.

Yadi frowned again, and this time I wasn't sure what he was trying to get across with his expression.

'As I was saying, you're going to change your mind.' I crossed my ankles. 'Do you know Tati S. Abdillah?'

'She's my mom, you idiot.'

That's the main difference between Spike and Pongo. Spike is so cute and childlike that I want to shove him off a cliff. Pongo, on the other hand, is so gruff and grating that causing his death is equally appealing.

'Correct. And this old chatterbox mother of yours is currently tied to a chair. I had her eat undercooked rice and then forced her to drink eight litres of water. Over the next few hours, the rice in her stomach will keep expanding until one of two things happens: she dies and then her stomach bursts, or her stomach bursts and she dies. Either way she's a goner, unless you go to her right now, and I'm the only one who knows how to remove all that rice from her belly. As you can guess . . .' I took the bottle of green tea out of my bag and sipped. The absinthe loosened my tongue, like it always does. 'I don't plan on sharing that information with you unless you change your mind.'

'Well, if that's true, thank god,' he answered flatly. Dammit. 'She's been alive for too long. Feels like this'd be a good time for her to go. And it's not as though we have a good relationship, not since she got sick with . . . ah, well, we're not sure what it is, really.'

Afif caught the drift of my plan and joined in, with gusto: she grabbed Yadi by the hair. 'Only the lowliest of deadbeats wouldn't defend their own family. Where's your sense of basic human decency, huh?'

Wow, not bad. I didn't expect her to talk that way. It was as if Afif were Margaret Thatcher—well, if Thatcher had taken too many tabs of acid and finally seen the light, or something like that.

'Let's see,' I said, unfolding the photo of Bachtiar. 'If you don't love your mom, maybe this will change your mind. Your father here, I buried him alive in my yard and stuck a straw in his mouth so he can keep breathing. The only way to save him is to change your mind.'

'Bury him twice, why don't you.'

Afif was really getting into it; she pulled Yadi's head so far back that anyone would have been tempted to flick his Adam's apple. 'You're crossing a line, you hear me? Just because you make your own money doesn't mean you ca—'

'The first time he was buried was 18 years ago.'

Afif and I glanced at each other.

Spotting the security guard outside, she quickly released Yadi's scalp.

'Then why did your mom say she was waiting for your dad to come home?'

'Your question explains why I decided not to live at home.'

'Oof. Fine. What do I have to do to make you change your mind?' I asked. 'We need an inside man.'

Afif shot me a look.

'What?' I said. 'You have to know somebody if you want to get anything done in this country.'

'Have you heard of the infamous village in Bangladesh that's a safe haven for thieves? The town's been an accessory to robbery for over 100 years.' Typical Yadi, dodging the question by telling a story. He repeated the phrase *100 years* before finally finishing his thought. 'And yet the villagers don't consider themselves thieves.'

'Don't exaggerate,' I said. 'We're doing this once. One time. It'll be great.'

'You don't get the point of the story. Stealing is a drug, and it only drags you down.'

As Yadi finished moralizing, Nurida emerged from the back of the store, mumbling under her breath. At first, she was muttering the sorts of things someone who's angry ordinarily says (and then some). Next came the value of the rupiah to the dollar, more muttering, names of schoolteachers, more of the usual angry words,

something about the educational system, reference pric-
ing rules for purchases and, finally, an enormous number.
She sounded like a steam train. Or maybe Eminem if he
were a middle-aged mom. I was impressed.

'If you don't get the money by next week, I want a
divorce.'

An even more impressive finale.

Without changing her tone, Nurida turned to me and
said, 'Wan Ali is out, taking a walk with his wife.'

I nodded. It's never a good idea to launch into explanations when people are angry. They only listen to what
they want to hear. And at that moment, I'd guess that
Nurida didn't want to hear anything except for a guar-
antee from her husband, so I just nodded in the hopes
that my nonverbal signs of agreement would discourage
her from going off again.

'I should've known you were broke,' I said to Yadi.

'Just because I'm broke doesn't mean I want to steal.'

'It's precisely because you're broke that you should
steal. That's how you'd make money.'

Yadi shook his head. 'I've already changed my mind.'

'Because you need the cash?'

He shook his head again. 'I could get by without
money my whole life, but I wouldn't survive if Nurida
left me.'

I wanted to puke and laugh at the same time. That
seemed difficult. Instead, I patted Yadi on the back twice,

trying to boost his self-confidence by telling him that his large frame concealed a fighting spirit that shone more brightly than the midday sun. 'You've got massive balls, my friend! Balls so big that I bet they're what move your arms and legs, not muscles and nerves.' Yadi didn't seem to have heard me, but Afif turned red.

'I'll help,' Yadi said, wiping down the counter, 'on one condition.'

'Why only one?' I replied. 'You underestimate me.'

Yadi squirted some more soap and wiped it off in a circular motion. 'I want my fair share.'

'The way you're approaching this conversation makes me think of a janitor at the mosque, but sure.' I opened my bag and caressed the two bars of soap inside. 'In your opinion, Yadi, is a robbery less sinful if the spoils are split equally?'

'I've heard—'

'We've all heard the story about the village of thieves. Do you want me to repeat it?'

'Who the hell cares.'

I handed him the bars of soap and explained that all he needed to do was duplicate the keys to the shop. 'And Agnes won't mind giving you 5 per cent of her share.'

Agnes glared at me. I could feel how badly she wanted to yank my hair, which is why I took two steps back.

'So, is your real name Afif or Agnes?' Yadi asked in all seriousness.

'Afif, obviously,' she answered. 'But you can call me Agnes, if you want. If you really want.'

'Get to know each other on your own time. Right now, we have to meet up with someone who can immobilize Wan Ali. I noticed a Startlet in your mom's garage. Does it still work?'

'It does. I'm always sneaking it out of the house, half the time to get the thing fixed. It was my dad's, so driving the car always makes me feel better, but the upkeep is wringing me dry.'

'Great. You have 15 minutes to copy the store key.' I lit a cigarette. 'We're leaving when I'm done smoking.'

Yadi exited the room without a word. He returned some 45 minutes later. I'd have punched him in the face had he not jingled the pockets of his pants. I suppressed my less noble urges and told him to gather his things.

'But I'm wo—'

'Forget about work,' I said. 'It's time to steal.'

Cortázar carried all three of us. I was steering, with Afif in the middle and Yadi at the back. We headed in the direction of that lying old crone. Damnit. I regretted feeling sorry for her and promising I'd help look for her husband. But still, part of me felt sympathy for her. The death of a loved one can distort everything around you. Grief becomes a funhouse mirror held centimetres away from your face, and no matter where you turn, a warped world reflects back at you. Sometimes the contortions get so bad you want to harm yourself, but everyone knows that doesn't do any good. Your only option is to act as though that mirror hasn't been pushed up against your nose and remark that the deceased will always be alive in your memories, in prayers, or as spirits, either curious on earth or resting peacefully in the afterlife.

Afif shifted her weight and Cortázar swayed. The steering wheel quivered, a sign that my passengers were getting nervous. I spurred Cortázar on, glanced over my shoulder, and informed her that the brakes failed. The quivering grew more pronounced as Cortázar enthusiastically charged forward. If there'd been a hill by the side of the road, I'd have turned up it sharply; adding a few rocks to the situation would've made things more interesting. But we were on a typical road, lined only by houses and shops and a pavement that looked as decrepit as a robot built back in 2076. Afif looped her arms around my waist, which made me uncomfortable. I let it slide, though, since she must have been petrified.

A black jeep with Semarang or Madura plates (the paint was flaking off, so the letters weren't legible from a distance) was just pulling away from Tati's house when we arrived. Yadi didn't recognize the car, and we were suspicious that the driver might've been a lover. Anything is possible. Yadi blanched when he heard me chirp the cliché that love knows no age. It wasn't my intention to say something so trite, but earlier I'd blurted out, 'Looks like Tati, that old-fart-who-reeks-of-the-angel-of-death's-armpits-every-time-she-opens-her-yap, is going through puberty again.' So, I added a saccharine statement as an apology. It was probably unnecessary, because Yadi had already walked over to the car in the garage and switched on the ignition without bothering to announce his presence to the owner of the house. Tati rushed outside and, releasing a high-pitched shriek that only old people are capable of, screeched: 'Thief!'

I need you to confirm this: there was no witness to your actions on the morning in question?

As I said, God is Our Witness.

I'll rephrase. No person can testify to your whereabouts three days ago, right?

I myself am a person, and I witnessed what I did. My eyesight is very good. It feels like you're implying that my vision is failing me, sir.

Fine. I'll try again. Other than yourself, no *person* witnessed what you were doing?

Ah, now that's accurate.

Did you see the victim that day?

We spent nearly the whole day together, if I remember correctly.

If that's the case, you're in big trouble. You could've easily planned the murder when you woke up and then carried out the crime later that same day. It's plausible that you poisoned the victim, for example.

If it were up to me, I'd say you've gone mad, but I suppose you're not wrong. That is technically possible.

Since no one can confirm your alibi, this drawn-out story you've been telling me is useless. My suspicions seem to be holding up.

What do you mean? Ah, I see. But I called the vegetable market.

Who knows if you're telling the truth?

Fine, let's go with your version of events. If there's one thing I've learned in life, it's that arguing with idiots is useless. It only makes stupidity multiply.

Are you implying something about my intelligence?

Not explicitly. You could say that I've given you advice, take it or leave it.

[Officer laughs.]

You call me stupid, but who's here to testify on your behalf? No one, right?

Except God.

Unfortunately, we can't ask God to come down to the station and give a statement right now.

I'm not sure what you mean, officer. God is everywhere.

Listen up. Here are the facts: that kid was healthy as a horse and then one day he up and dies. Unexpected heart attacks are possible, especially when you take into consideration lifestyle and other contextual factors, but it's not out of the question that someone killed him and made it look like natural causes. And you'd know how. You've written all about your experiences as a cardiologist, in your memoir.

Correct. You're entirely correct. Sometimes I miss that phase of my life, even though I wasn't very happy. People came to me with their ailments, and I helped them as best I could—that is to say, in some cases nothing could be done, and that's life.

As for the boy who died, yes, these things happen even to those in good health. Remember the rabbits? They were doing fine the day before they passed.

So, you don't deny that you have expertise on heart conditions.

How could I, if I put it in writing?

You're confirming my hunch. I'm convinced antidepressants were slipped into the victim's drink. Correct me if I'm wrong, but antidepressants shrink blood vessels, a fact that a cardiologist such as yourself would be aware of. Besides, we found *this* at your house.

That's mine. Sir Shakur's son gives me the pills, his assistant delivers them. He told me to take one capsule a day.

Can you state on the record that the medicine was in your possession three days ago?

Come on, I already told you it's mine, and you found the bottle in my home. What do you actually want to ask me?

All I want is confirmation that these pills are yours. Is that correct?

It feels like you should be capable of recognizing a lie. Oh my . . . You're talking in circles and, frankly, it's making me feel cornered.

You wouldn't feel that way if you'd done nothing wrong.

It's not about what I've done, officer, it's your questions. There's something off about how you're asking me things, but I'm not well versed in the methods of police questioning, so I have to assume that you're being professional. In my own career, I've had to maintain decorum, so I think I understand the position you're in right now.

Moving on. According to my report, you had someone else over after the victim left your house. Is that correct?

Yes. A man wearing a mask. A very ugly mask if I recall. Instead of making him seem suave, he looked a bit like a toad.

Did you hire that man to trail the victim?

Why would I do that?

To check if the poison worked. You hired him to kill the victim.

Not that I'm aware of.

I'm not finished.

Fine.

I have reason to believe that the man who came to your house is a hitman.

That would explain the mask.

You don't seem surprised.

Why would I be? It's not shocking that a hitman would want to hide his identity.

I've come up with a little theory based on our chat. Four days ago, you wake up at dawn and see that your husband isn't in bed. He didn't come home the night before. You suspect that the victim is implicated in your husband's absence. Maybe he's the son of your husband's new female friend. I'm basing this on that offhand comment you made: 'I had the sneaking suspicion that I'd met the young man before. The face was familiar.' With that, I surmise that you knew the victim, or at the very least you'd met him before the day in question, a fact you've been trying to hide. The victim comes over to your house and you try to force a confession about what your husband is up to. But he doesn't crack. So maybe you strike a deal: if he really doesn't know where your husband is, he should be able to take you to his family's house, no problem. But unexpectedly, all he does is drive you around in circles. Realizing the dirty trick some

73

snot-nosed kid tried to pull on you, you slip the victim those antidepressants. And just to be sure the deed is done, you hire that hitman to check up on your target. What do you think, do you have a defence?

You should start writing detective stories, officer. Your talents might be of better use in that area, considering that most crime novels I've read start out by trying to confuse the reader—and they're all by different authors, mind you. I'm very confused by this theory of yours, and that's a compliment. I had some choice words for you, but it occurred to me that rather than swear, it would make more sense to advise you on how to channel your skillset in a more constructive direction.

Are you confirming my theory?

Oh, the call to prayer. I need to pray.

That's the ringtone from my colleague's cell phone.

And yet prayer is still prayer, officer.

—END OF AUDIO FILE—

Compression cylinder

Metal shard
(sharpened to a
45-degree angle)

Manual pump (to be
used in case of a jam
or malfunction)

Trigger

Vial of dry ice

Constructed from spare parts and scrap metal, this lethal weapon relies on physics. The pressure from the sublimated dry ice launches a small iron cylinder with a bevelled metal shard attached to the front end. When the tip pierces your skin, you only feel a quick, sharp, painful prick at first, something like a fire-ant bite. Next comes an ice-cold shock, and then pain spreads steadily as the diameter of the wound expands. No need to worry, though—these steps usually happen in quick succession. The handle of the weapon is wrapped in cloth to reduce the risk of its owner leaving fingerprints.

04

Sixteen and a half hours to go before the heist, with Cortázar, Afif, Yadi and Tati as my accomplices. And yet moments ago, we found ourselves wrapped up in a tiresome squabble.

'No, none of this has anything to do with my mom leaving her medical practice and getting into Adnan Oktar's crank theories, that's none of my business. The problem is, she's not in her right mind. No, not because she's senile, not because of Alzheimer's either. She chooses not to remember certain things. It all started with Lazarus, dammit. Have you all heard the story?'

Yadi recounted how Lazarus had been brought back to life with Jesus's help. His mother was a similar figure, resuscitated, but without the son of God. Lazarus syndrome.

With a huffy sigh, he launched into his story.

It all started with a phone call. Yadi came home one Friday from dawn prayers to find his mother slumped by the phone, face smeared with porridge. The receiver was dangling by its cord, a blue bowl had been knocked onto the floor, and the sound of a man's voice midway through a drastic analysis on the value of the dollar crackled from a portable radio. Yadi checked his mother's pulse and breathing before calling an ambulance. The line was busy.

'I drove her to the hospital myself, but I knew it was too late. The doctor, chagrined, offered me his condolences twice. First, for the death of my father, and second, for my mother's passing. My father was killed in a car crash, and my mother's heart stopped beating when she heard the news. Twenty minutes passed,' Yadi paused to make that tsk sound, his Adam's apple rising and falling as though he was trying to ingest something that refused to be swallowed, 'and then my mother came back to life. Suspended animation.'

According to the doctor, none of Tati's internal organs had been damaged during the many minutes that blood had stopped flowing through her veins. It took a full day for her to regain consciousness, and then another before Yadi broke the news of his father's death. When he did, Tati froze like a dead lizard. 'I tried to get her to say something, but she acted as though couldn't hear me. She only started speaking after I finished telling her what happened. And you know what she said to me?'

I shook my head.

'Devil child!' Yadi exclaimed, imitating the expression on his mother's face when she uttered the same phrase. 'She called me that because I'd said my father was dead.'

'He really is an evil boy,' Tati walked over to us, cutting Yadi off. 'He had the gall to wish death on his father. But I realize now that maybe I'm to blame. I raised him, after all.'

'See?' Yadi said. 'And this sickness of hers has been getting worse. When I got married, she refused to give me her blessing. She was waiting to consult dad. After that, I moved out and went to live with my aunt. But I come home once a week to fix up the car. It's the first car I ever drove, full of memories.'

Tati mumbled a sentence so long that it was incomprehensible, then kept grumbling even once everyone else had stopped talking.

I clapped Yadi on the shoulder. 'All right, let's brainstorm. How should the plan—'

'Have you heard about the arrogant Chinese general who lost a war because he kept secrets from his advisors? You've also held your cards pretty close to your chest.'

'I certainly have, and I bet you've heard plenty of stories that end with the phrase, "everything turned out all right in the end". That's how my plans always go, so don't force me to repeat the cliché or my mouth will fall asleep. Before I reveal our next steps, I need to know who's a friend. You're not to be trusted quite yet.'

'How about the story of a man so irritating that he never had any friends? You're that man, and I have no interest in your friendship.'

I got in his face and whispered, 'Have you heard about a broke husband whose wife decides to leave him?'

'Whatever.' Yadi took a step back. 'The batshit old crone can tag along. And let's be clear, I'm doing this for Ida.'

'Devil child,' I snorted. 'Do it as an offering to the Queen of the South Sea for all I care. If you want to convince me of your loyalty, your first task is to make your mother shut up before we have a problem with the neighbours.'

Just like that, they stopped bickering. Afif and I sped off on Cortázar; Yadi trailed us in the Starlet, Tati beside him in the passenger seat. Keeping my eyes on the road, I asked Afif when she thought they'd last sat in such close proximity. Some 10 or 20 years ago, Afif guessed. A difference of 10 years makes for a terrible estimate, I said, and told her to pick one or the other. Instead, she went on about how the number didn't matter, since they were next to each other now, which was heart-warming either way. I spent the rest of the drive contemplating the word *heart-warming*. I imagined someone opening up their chest, pulling out their heart, patting it dry, then setting it behind the refrigerator or near a stove. We made a few more turns and then arrived at the Flying Monster, Jethro's auto shop.

Cortázar pulled into the shop, and I walked towards Yadi, who looked stunned as he gazed at the water buffalo skulls adorning the shop's sign. His car radio was playing 'Datanglah' by Chrisye, Cortázar's favourite song. When he refuses to start his engine, I play the clip on my cell phone for encouragement. Yadi asked me something as he took off his seatbelt, but I wasn't listening. The last bars of 'Datanglah' faded into a jingle, followed by a radio announcer gushing out a greeting. One of his colleagues joined him to read out the headlines in alternating sentences: NASA predicts that in the next decade, a meteor two times the size of Earth will be visible in the northern hemisphere. The first announcer, the one whose voice sounded like Tony Leung's, cracked a joke by singing the chorus of 'I Don't Wanna Miss a Thing', which made me think of *Armageddon*, then Michael Bay's smiling face. What a dumbass. The announcer chuckled but stopped suddenly when his companion mentioned the possibility that the meteor might collide with Earth. Silence, just for a second, before Tony Leung made another ill-advised attempt at a joke. I'd almost made it to the punchline when Yadi switched off the stereo. 'What is this place, a body shop or a witch doctor's house?'

*

I met Jethro six years ago. One August night, I left the hospital and walked to a nearby bridge for some fresh air. The canal below had just been cleared of debris; the backhoe was still parked by the banks. I skimmed a newspaper in the dim cast of streetlights while sipping at a strawberry juice that I'd bought at a fast-food joint.

The air smelled like dried mud. I heard a noise very close by, a loud *sploosh* that sounded something like a whale carcass being heaved into the canal.

A few minutes later, a man wearing a red jacket appeared, illuminated by a nearby lamppost. Soaking wet, he reminded me of a feral cat. He dashed Dashing across the street, gave me a quick glance, then scrambled up the bank of the canal and jumped. There it was again: *sploosh*. I glanced down below; the water's slow current belied its depth, and the area had just been cleaned—any rods, planks of wood, bamboo or large stones would've been removed. If this guy was trying to kill himself, he'd chosen the wrong place. Enola Gay would have to drop Little Boy from the bridge for this suicide attempt to work. I speculated that he must enjoy jumping off tall structures in his spare time—plenty of those types these days. The man appeared again on the other side of the street, soaked and dismal. He hurried across the street, gave me that look, and jumped yet again. *Sploosh*.

He emerged on the other side of the road and repeated the cycle yet again, but this time, he paused on the bank of the canal. I couldn't help but stare, even though I was trying to stay out of the situation. His leather jacket had a red-and-blue capsule embroidered on the back. An imitation of the outfit worn by Shotaro Kaneda, leader of the Capsule Gang in *Akira*. The difference being that this guy wasn't about to lead anyone anywhere.

'You aren't gonna stop me from killing myself?'

I picked my nose while processing that I'd been wrong, he wasn't an adrenaline junkie. It felt premature to categorize him as a simpleton though. He could be crazy, since he was doing the same thing over and over, expecting a different result. 'Killing yourself is a tough decision, especially after picking out shoes that don't clash with that jacket. I'm guessing you've thought long and hard about this. Your choice, none of my business.'

As though he was after a ball of yarn, he slid down from the canal and darted past me towards Cortázar, who was parked under a broken lamppost. 'Binter Merzy, 1976 model. Modified to brat style. Maroon paint with a touch of chrome on the head and taillights, exhaust pipes, and combustion chamber. Nice. Your bike?'

'It's not a bike, exactly,' I answered. 'Call him Cortázar.'

'You've got decent taste,' he said, walking over to me. He held out his hand. 'Jethro.'

Jethro's skin tone reminded me of the clay lining the banks of Jakarta's waterways, lending credibility to the notion that God created Adam from earth. And you know how God must've formed this guy's nose? My guess is that one day, the Almighty bit into a guava next to a pot of Jethro dough, but the guava had gone bad. So, God tossed the fruit into the pot, and the sight of it half-submerged inspired him: 'Hm, this could be my model for a nose,' and so it was. But if you ask me, Jethro had no negative qualities other than his name, which is a mouthful. When I shook his outstretched hand, I told him as much and asked if I could call him Njet instead. Simpler. He agreed, and then told me a story.

'A friend of mine owns a body shop that's barely staying afloat. The car industry is doing well, but when clients go to the shop, they always ask for services on credit, and that screws a small business. Then, last week, this friend proposes to the girl of his dreams, but she turns him down because of religious differences. His girlfriend is Catholic, my friend's a Jehovah's Witness. Mainstream Christians think Jehovah's Witnesses are quacks. Heretical, they call them, or mock them as losers and tell them get lost if they proselytize. So, this girlfriend finds out that my buddy is a Jehovah's Witness and gets all distant, saying she wants to break up even though she'd been the one pressuring him about marriage in the first place. Eventually, my friend goes home and thinks long and hard about his life. He's the type who's always down on his luck, and he starts to wonder, why go on living if life itself seems to reject you at every turn?'

Just as I was starting to feel for the guy in the story, Njet buttoned up his jacket and said: 'The friend I'm describing is me.'

I objected, explaining that there's no need to talk about yourself in the third person. 'It makes the story seem sadder,' he replied.

I gave Njet a ride home. As time went on, he became Cortázar's mechanic and the business at his body shop quadrupled. He thanked me, claiming I was his good-luck charm. In my head, I returned the sentiment; no mechanic other than Njet could handle Cortázar. Sure, they could fix an engine and that sort of thing, but they weren't able to make Cortázar happy. Only two people in this world can convince Cortázar not to stall in the middle of the road: Kik and Njet.

Kik and Njet had started dating. After she broke up with me, and then slapped me, the natural course of events played out. Kik poured her heart out to Njet, telling him about her pregnancy, about how I wasn't the kind of man who assumed responsibility for my actions, how I wasn't a good friend, and so on. Then Njet's dopey demeanour and his stories about the misery he'd experienced—narrated in the third person—made Kik fall in love. At first, I thought Njet was trying to be funny in a self-deprecating way. But Kik herself told me that Njet didn't make her laugh. He let her see a man by her side who was a real human being, not a manipulative monster who happened to walk on two legs like me. Njet was able to be vulnerable, which made Kik feel safe. Once her disgust towards me dissipated, Kik and I were back on speaking terms. Still, ever since we had that first conversation about her and Njet, my perspective on humour shifted a bit, especially when it comes to televised stand-up. I started wondering, what if I'd been wrong all along, and something is a lot funnier when no one laughs at the punchline? I decided to leave it at that and didn't mull over the problem any further.

When I heard that Kik and Njet were dating and talking about marriage, I wanted to spread the joy before I overdosed on emotion. Kik was a Muslim, Njet a Jehovah's Witness. Not a problem, as far as family went, since Kik's parents disowned her when they found out that she'd gotten knocked up, and Njet wasn't the kind of person who cared to ask mom and pop for their blessing. The bigger issue was that neither bride nor groom-to-be had money. Kik was carrying my child, and in a few short months it would look like she'd swallowed a pillow. I wasn't concerned about the optics; a wedding with no relatives in attendance seemed unnecessary, and even if they felt that some sort of celebration was called for, I'd be the sole guest. Whatever. The thing that bugged me was how Njet followed up his invitation: 'After the honeymoon's over, you wouldn't want your child to be raised on motor oil instead of milk, would you, Gaspar?'

*

Njet was right. That's why I'd stopped by the shop that afternoon, to offer him a path towards financial security: get in on the robbery, Njet. All you need is a bit of nerve.

I pulled him aside after giving Afif the task of trapping Kik in a conversation so that we could talk uninterrupted.

'Sure, sounds great in theory, but you're not in my position here.'

'Come on. Remember when you stood up to Kik's father despite that formidable beard of his?' I asked, referencing the night of Njet's proposal. Everything got awkward after he admitted to being a Christian. Njet, loyal as ever, had got up from his seat and asserted himself: 'What kind of father do you think you are, disowning her? You may have raised this woman, but she's capable of making her own decisions.' Impressive.

'I had no choice. You were pressing Koka to my back,' Njet said under his breath.

Koka is our invention, the first and only steampunk weapon we ever successfully engineered. The size of a Glock, but with a longer barrel, it's made from a one-centimetre-diameter plumbing tube, a fire-extinguisher valve and a small vial filled with dry ice. Fire it up and the dry ice sublimates so that the valve can open with enough air pressure to shoot rubber bullets, or even shards of metal up to half an inch long.

'Frankly, there are two reasons why you should be jumping at this opportunity,' I said, then glanced towards Afif, Tati, Yadi and Kik to confirm that they were still busy talking. 'I couldn't care less if you and Kik skip into the sunset without a penny, but it's not as though you can solder a car battery onto my kid's stomach to make sure he won't go hungry. That's reason number one. And you'll only ask to hear the second if you want nightmares for a week. So, tell me, would you rather be terrorized by sleepless nights or give a bit more thought to an offer that'll make everyone happy?'

Njet was silent. I batted my tongue against the top of my mouth while gauging his reaction.

'So?' I asked, doubtful.

Njet hung his head. 'I can't even imagine what happiness looks like.'

I clapped him on the back. I was tempted to reply by invoking God but decided it'd only complicate matters further. 'Too late, time's up. Just tag along. Won't do any harm.'

'Are you about to die or something?'

'If that were the case, would you come with?'

'I'd think about it.'

'Okay, let's just say I'm going to die tomorrow.'

'And what happens if you don't?'

'Whatever doesn't kill me tomorrow will get me eventually, Njet.'

Njet smacked my head. 'You're the smartest person I know, Gaspar, and you have plenty of money. I don't get it, one day you tell your girlfriend to start dating me, the next you're asking me to commit a robbery with some elderly woman who's slower than a sloth. Where's all of this going?'

I put my arm around Njet's shoulder, leading him back to the group. 'It's all about the black box,' I said.

—TRANSCRIPT IV—

[Silence for 10 minutes. The witness prays. The investigator mutters quietly. Uneven breathing, footsteps, and fingers tapping the table are also audible.]

I'll admit I crossed a line with my last questions. Why don't you explain in your own words why you had contact with the victim that afternoon? But this time, please be brief.

Fine, though it's not like I have any choice. Here's how it happened: three days ago, I restocked all the coffee grounds in my house.

Coffee grounds?

That's right. My husband says that coffee absorbs smells. Back when I used the house for my medical practice, the whole place smelled like a hospital, which bothered my husband. One day, when we were at the market, he bought a kilo of ground coffee. That was odd—he's a tea drinker—so I asked him what he was up to. Smiling, he didn't answer. 'You'll see,' he said.

He also started picking out little bowls. He asked me which ones I liked better, the blue or the red, and I answered blue. He bought around two dozen. I started thinking that maybe he'd cooked up the idea for a small business venture, a coffee stall or something of the sort, but that wasn't it. When we got home, he filled all those little bowls with coffee and placed them in every corner of the house. He put four in the room we used for my practice, now that's our storage space. When I looked at him quizzically, he explained that this little trick would get rid of that hospital smell, or at least make it less over-powering. That's how I figured out that my husband is sensitive to certain aromas, and ever since, I've been sure to go around the house refilling the dishes at least once a week, every two weeks at the most. Sorry, what was the question?

I asked you to tell me what led you to meet with the victim. Succinctly.

Ah, yes. Three days ago, I was refreshing the dishes of ground coffee I keep in my house, since my husband claims that the beans get rid of strong odours. The space reeked of medicine back when worked out of my house. We'd gone shopping one day and he grabbed a whole kilo of coffee and some little bowls too, blue ones, because I said I liked them best. He bought around two dozen of those dishes! I was sure it was his entrepreneurial mind at work and imagined he'd launch a successful coffee stand. But when we got home, he filled those little bowls with the coffee and placed them all around the house, especially in the storage room—see, that's where I used to run my practice. Puzzled, I watched him, and that's when he told me what he was doing. Ground coffee would make the hospital smell go away. I had no idea my husband was so averse to the scent of medicine, but once I found out, I made sure to regularly change out the coffee. That morning, it occurred to me that the chore had slipped my mind. I'm getting old, you know how it is. So, I went about restocking the coffee grounds, starting in the living room, making my way through the house.

I was almost done when I realized that a lightbulb had gone out. Fortunately, I keep a few extras on hand. I used to change bulbs myself, but once I fell off the stepstool and hit my head, so my husband said it should be one of his chores. As I said before, my husband hadn't come home yet, and I didn't like how dark the bathroom was. Moist, dark, damp places make me think about death. So, I went to ask a neighbour for help and circled the block without seeing a soul. As I stood outside of my house, a young man and his friend approached me and offered to help. If I'm not mistaken, that's the first time I saw the boy.

But earlier you said that you recognized him.

Yes, that's right. His face seemed familiar, which is why I said I *felt as though* we'd met before. I'm not completely sure.

Make an effort to remember.

I've been trying way before you asked me to. Doesn't do any good.

Fine. Explain what happened after the victim helped you change the lightbulb.

We chatted a bit in the living room.

Then?

He left. Not long after, the masked man paid me a visit. The gaps framing his eyes were winged at the tips, and the area around the mouth was open so he could talk, snack on nuts and sample the sweet drink that I offered him, all without showing his face.

Describe the mask in more detail.

I'm having a hard time putting it into words, but I can picture it as clear as day. The fabric was pink, and then certain areas were decorated with thin blue embroidery, like around the eyes and mouth.

Why would you allow this stranger to enter your home?

First of all, I don't judge people based on appearances. Also, I asked him to take off his mask when we met.

You saw his face?

Oh my, what else could there possibly be behind that mask?

What did he look like?

I forget what his features were like, but broadly speaking, his head was like a hardboiled egg with a crack down the middle.

What did the two of you talk about?

He asked me how I was doing. He claimed we already knew each other, that he was a former patient of mine. I was having a hard time placing him, so he told me about the night we met. He'd grown up on the streets, his mother and father died without leaving him a cent. It's not as though he enjoyed arm wrestling for money, he explained, but if he wanted to survive, what choice did he have? That night he'd been trying to get something to eat and stopped by a local bar. He didn't have even a penny to gamble with, so he suggested a different kind of bet: if he won, he'd take a thousand rupiah, but if he lost, he'd swallow four live cockroaches, without even a sip of water to help wash them down. With a nod, his competitor agreed and sent the bartender to go hunt down a few roaches by the toilet. The masked man lost. Having forced the four critters down his throat, he said he'd repeat the challenge, this time with higher stakes. The bartender had found ten cockroaches; four were in his stomach, six were left, and he bet on finishing them off. His opponent agreed. And once again, the masked man's arm wrestling failed him. He kept betting again and again, until . . . until his challenger, with a smirk, reminded him that those cockroaches weren't dead. We're talking about a bug that can stay alive inside pipes and sewers, thrive in nuclear waste—what, you think they're about to die in a human throat? The masked man had no reason to take his competitor's word, but he started getting nervous anyway. The question echoed in his head until he felt tiny legs scaling his oesophagus. He sprinted to the toilet and tried to force himself to vomit. No luck. Panicking, he grabbed a bottle of floor cleaner and chugged. The bartender found him doubled over the toilet and took him to my clinic, which was closer than any hospital. The man could have died if the bartender had tried to drive him all that way. The masked man told me that he never forgets people who've seen his face, not even after 15 years have gone by, not even if their appearance has changed.

Did you take off his mask at the time?

I must have, but I can't remember. If everything he told me is true, the first thing I would've done is remove his mask to help him breathe.

And you can't recall any details about his face?

This happened a long time ago. I've seen a lot of faces. Even your face seems familiar, sir. If I think about it, your bone structure makes me think of George Clooney, but your chin is a lot like Tommy Soeharto's.

Sure. What else did you and this man discuss three days ago?

After the story, he asked what I'd been chatting about with the two kids who just stopped by. I told him, in all honestly, that we didn't discuss anything important. They helped me change a lightbulb and promised to help my husband find his way home. Then I showed them my old photo albums, like I always do for guests, since I adore telling the stories I've jotted down on the back of each picture. The pair then said goodbye and shook my hand. The girl had sweaty palms, I noticed. Maybe she has a heart condition.

You didn't sense anything unusual about the masked man? Most people pay close attention when strangers enter their homes.

Nothing was out of the ordinary. He didn't act like a stranger. He behaved as though he were my own son, actually. He was articulate, polite, knowledgeable. In those respects, he reminded me a bit of my husband, and that's why I showed him my photo album. He listened to my stories without interrupting me. Well, with one exception . . .

When was that?

It happened when I took out a picture of my husband with my brother-in-law. The masked man asked about the black box. Wait a minute, if I remember correctly, the couple that stopped by also took an interest in that box, especially the young man.

Why does everyone care so much about this box? Who owns it?

I wish I could explain why people are so interested in that damn thing, but I'm myself not sure why. I only know a little bit ab—[*static for 10 minutes*]—fell into Crassus's hands. That evil man had managed to snatch the black box from a Syrian man nam—[*static for 20 seconds*]—ake himself rich.

Some say the black box also allowed Moses, the King of Mali, to travel to Mecca for the Hajj. He set out on his journey with tens of thousands of soldiers and slaves, passing through Algeria and Egypt. The cost is nothing to scoff at, officer, given that the journey took an entire year. Imagine the quantity of gold and supplies he must have carried with him. According to my brother-in-law, Moses sacrificed a great sum to fund this trip to the Hajj. If you were to estimate how expensive that would be today, I'd guess it'd amount to more than 100 trillion rupiah. Where could he have gotten that much money? The story has a happy ending too. He returned in good health and with the title of haji, even though his country went bankrupt.

The box was then passed from one person to the next until it finally fell into the hands of Mir Osman Ali Khan, who—[*static for 40 seconds*]—now owned by my little sister's husband. He was the one who told me this back-story. He's stingy and irritating, yes, but I appreciate the tales he tells. Maybe it's true that people of Arab descent are excellent storytellers.

In other words, everything you know about this black box is based on rumours.

Well, yes.

Has it occurred to you that your brother-in-law could've made it all up?

Oh, that's definitely possible. But I don't care, so long as the plot is good. In any case, I never accepted any of his help, so if the story of the black box is a lie and he really amassed a small fortune making deals with jinn as people say, I wouldn't have sinn—[*static for 30 seconds*]—eighbour of mine once said Wan Ali is indebted to those spirits. That's why he keeps renovating his house each September. When the jinn come to collect their money, he can say, 'How could I possibly give you money? Look around, I'm in the middle of fixing up my house.' I think my neighbour's right. She has a child who can see spirits, and one day, they went to Wan Ali's jewellery store on a busy afternoon. The kid started screaming, begging not to be taken inside. My neighbour asked what was wrong, and the child replied: 'Don't you see all the monkeys and the spiders?' In those innocent eyes, Wan Ali's clients were all demon monkeys and spiders. Children are pure, they see things when none of the rest of us can.

I can't believe that you're telling me this—you, a former doctor!

I hardly believe it myself. How could we be fooled by the devil for nearly half a century? By the way, can I make a call? I want to check if my husband's home.

—END OF AUDIO FILE—

96

BABAJI

Thirty-six large spikes
Thirty-six is the atomic number for Krypton, a word that comes from the Greek kryptos, which means 'that which is hidden'.

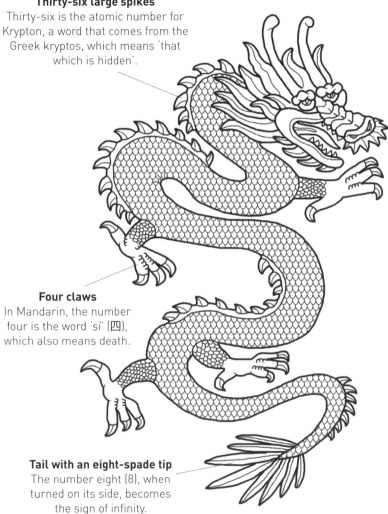

Four claws
In Mandarin, the number four is the word 'si' (四), which also means death.

Tail with an eight-spade tip
The number eight (8), when turned on its side, becomes the sign of infinity.

05

Cortázar, Afif, Yadi and Tati are set to join the robbery. With a mere 16 hours to go, I tried to convince Kik and Njet to get in on the plan by revealing my motive for the crime.

I first heard about the black box through Babaji, my father's driver. The one before him had been sacked after attempting to steal my dad's beloved Mercy Tiger. Babaji was a man of South Asian origin, bald save for some hair running from his ears to the top of his neck. He kept his beard well groomed, moustache and sideburns neatly trimmed. If you stood close to him, you could catch a whiff of a powerful smell, something like cat poop, but in a good way. Babaji was discrete; without saying a word, he'd give rides to the woman my father was having an affair with, as well as the man my mother had started seeing. He was around for most of my childhood. Once, when my parents got into a big fight, I stood there, slack-jawed and staring at the words forming on my parents' lips, and Babaji came over and put his arm around me. In a low voice he said, 'If you're ever in a tough situation, just click your tongue against the roof of your mouth. Time will feel like it's moving faster, and eventually your problems will go away on their own.'

He demonstrated how I should shape my lips in order to make the sound and, as I focused on trying to produce a click, told me a story: 'A long, long time ago, the people who lived in the village at the foot of Govardhan Hill made an offering to the god Indra, asking him to bring rain.'

Indra grew arrogant from power, and Krishna decided to teach him a lesson. He told the people of the village that instead of giving offerings to Indra, they should dedicate themselves to Govardhan, the hill that collected water when Indra didn't bring the rain to nourish the grasses that their cattle would feed on.

Indra lost his temper and unleashed a torrential downpour lasting seven days and seven nights. Krishna protected the villagers by lifting Govardhan Hill with his pinky finger, which shielded the village for the duration of the storm. On the fifth day of rain, Achal, a farmer who had been hiding under the shadow of the hill, spotted a black box half-buried in the ground. At first, he assumed it was an unremarkable stone, but its unusual shape made him think twice. He had a lot of free time on his hands, waiting around for the rain to let up, so he decided to dig the object out of the earth. 'The box was magical. You know why?' Babaji said in a cadence that reminded me of a slow-moving stream. He spoke softly but his voice, deep and rich, commanded my full attention until the volume of my mom and dad's argument was reduced to that of a mosquito buzzing around my ear.

I shook my head, still attempting to tap the roof of my mouth with my tongue.

'Because it contains all the knowledge in the universe.'

I nodded, hypnotized.

'The box was passed from owner to owner for over 50 generations. Rumour has it, it's somewhere in Indonesia. That's why I'm in Jakarta,' Babaji continued, arm still around me. 'If you want, we can look for it together. Then, we can share the box's powers and you can use it to help your mom and dad stop fighting.'

I produced my first resonant click right as my mom, or maybe my dad, hurled an ashtray at the TV. 'I want to know what's inside the box,' I said.

'It'll be grand,' he said. An outdated expression, but I didn't bat an eye. Babaji said that sort of thing all the time.

'If you're serious about starting your search, here's where you should begin.'

Babaji handed me the detective novel *There's No Mystery in an Abandoned House* by Artur Harahap. Harahap was the kind of author revered in literary circles; his name was referenced repeatedly in Soleh Solihun's recent interview with critic Goenawan Mohammad, printed in *Playboy*. The book was thick, but I had spare time to kill after my parents' divorce. My mom asked my school to let me stay home for a while, and during the weeks I wasn't in class, my parents would take turns going on excursions with me. I read the novel while stepping into the gondola at the amusement park, standing in front of the elephant exhibit at the zoo, waiting in line at the cinema, lying next to the swimming pool, sitting in front of the judge during divorce proceedings. I discovered I could transform the courtroom into an abandoned house, just like the one the protagonist sneaks into in the novel.

The protagonist is 35 years old. He works as a private eye at night, after his nine-to-five job as a mid-level state bureaucrat. Most people in Indonesia think abandoned houses are full of remarkable, creepy mysteries, and everyone likes to talk about how what happened in this one would make your skin crawl, or about the savage acts that were carried out in that other one. Harahap's protagonist cracks the case of that hype. Alone, he enters empty homes to record videos of what happens there at night. He walks into nine infamously haunted houses and, in each, proves that nothing mysterious is going on; no ghosts, no staircases that extend infinitely, no piano that plays itself at night. The uncanny stories hanging over the houses are what make us convinced there's something inside. In reality, there's nothing, save some furniture draped in plastic, cobwebs, and a bit of odd-smelling mould or moss collecting in corners rarely graced by the light of day. The sound of footsteps, a figure that looks like a face in the dark, sudden move-ments in the shadows—all are mere projections of exist-ing fears. At the end of each investigation, our detective pulls down his pants and moons the camera.

'Until the tenth house,' I said and took a breath.

'Hold on,' Kik cut me off. 'You really read this book?'

I nodded. 'Yeah. Why?'

'Looks like you've been a deadbeat since you were a kid,' Kik announced. 'I read that novel at a used book-shop once, it's close to a thousand pages long. And all the narrator does in the first few chapters is roast the other characters, it's childish. The cases he chooses are bullshit. I can't think of a single interesting thing to say about the plot. But somehow, you liked it, which makes me think the novel was written specifically for people like you.'

'What do you mean, people like me?'

'You know . . .' Kik stroked her chin. 'You know, like you.'

'Like what? Like a monkey? A rusty razorblade? A broken radio? Like—'

'It would take me much longer than 24 hours to lay this out for you,' Kik interrupted. 'I know you too well, Gaspar. You're a clown. You entertain yourself like a buf-foon. Kermit the Frog, Count von Count, Unyil, Dufan, a jester at a child's birthday party. In a way, I feel lucky to have met someone like that in the flesh.'

'Wow. So fortunate! And meanwhile, it seems I barely know myself at all.'

Kik was ready to lunge at my throat, but in a rather father-like fashion Njet intervened and asked me to finish what I was saying.

Until the tenth house. The protagonist comes across a box. A black box, sitting on a coffee table in one of these abandoned houses. Torn between a deep desire to open the lid and the feeling that he really shouldn't, the detective bites his nails, undecided, and sits down on the sofa to think. He's cradling the box in his palm when, suddenly, a wave of fear sweeps over him. He sprints out of the house and leaves the box behind. Thoughts of the box haunt him that night and he can't sleep a wink. In his office the next day, guesses about what might've been inside run through his mind. What if there'd been part of a human head or a dead cat? Maybe it was unremarkable, some random documents, or entirely empty. Theories plague him until he decides to go back to the house and settle the matter. But when he sneaks inside, the box is gone.

'And that's basically how the novel ends. Only the best authors can hold a reader's attention like Harahap. The length of the book is irrelevant.'

I stretched out my legs and lit a cigarette, exhaling a cloud of smoke.

Yadi put his hands on his hips. 'The character's an idiot, don't you think? He must be jumping for joy, free to hypothesize about the black box for the rest of his days.'

'How could such a disobedient child know anything about joy?' Tati said.

'I can tell you a thing or two about happiness,' Yadi leaned his face towards Tati's. 'It's what you feel when you don't live anywhere near your mother.'

Afif pulled Yadi back by his hair, an activity she seemed to enjoy. 'You might feel justified saying things like that, but don't you dare try it while I'm around.'

'Go ahead, hate each other as much as you want, but only after we get away with the crime,' I said. 'And not a minute sooner.'

'Wait,' Afif said. 'You haven't finished your story.'

I'd just turned eight when I finished the novel. The judge ruled that I'd live with my mother, which meant I couldn't spend very much time with Babaji. I resented the decision, but there was no way around it: I'd have to wait until I turned 12 before I'd have any say in my living situation. So, I was shuffled into a new house, with a new dad, where I lived for four years until I moved back to my old home, reunited with Babaji. My dad was hardly ever around; he and his new wife decided to live outside the city. At first, he'd often drive in to see me, maybe three times a week. Then, gradually, he visited less and less—once a week, three times a month, once a month, eight times a year, once a year.

The Harahap novel was what first made me dream of becoming a detective. Babaji loved to go on about crime fiction. He said that from everything he'd read, he was able to suss out all the rules: if you want to write a good detective story, you should first hone the skill of confusing your reader. Then, your detective can swoop in like Jesus, playing the saviour who will parse through all the puzzles that you yourself designed, offering logical explanations that, even if they don't fully satisfy your reader, will at least make them sigh in relief from achieving some amount of clarity. Second: the detectives you invent don't need to be striking characters; they seem impressive by virtue of the intriguing incidents the author crafts for them to investigate. Murder, robbery, stalking, a grandfather clock with the ability to speak. They explore the kinds of places you'd rarely find in this country and meet beautiful women who don't exist in real life. I've concluded that Babaji was right, and if you don't mind me adding to his analysis, I'd say that crime fiction also imagines a world with one definitive version of the truth, simplifying the concepts of good and evil. In areas of the city filled with bad people, you can always find some reserve of goodness, that sort of thing. Not that I thought very hard about any of this when I was little. But in Babaji's opinion, Harahap's novel changed what it meant to be a private eye, because suddenly, you have a detective who doesn't determine what's true and what's false, who doesn't investigate gruesome crimes, and who never points his finger at the criminal. Detectives can be people who simply search for information, uncovering secrets. My dad has a camcorder, I told Babaji, I'm allowed to use it whenever I want. 'If that's so, let's be detectives next week, just like in the book.'

The first house I snuck into wasn't abandoned. A girl my age lived there (I was still eight at the time). She asked me what I was doing in her living room, and I told her I was a private eye. She replied that she liked detectives, which implied that she liked me too. But I can't do my job while you're still in the house, I said. She asked if she should leave. I nodded, saying that it wasn't a bad idea. So, she left me alone in her living room.

After poking about and filming some nooks and crannies, I went outside. The little girl was talking to Babaji. She said that she was usually home alone all afternoon; her parents worked at a store. Then she informed me that if I ever needed an empty house to investigate, I was welcome to come back. She'd play outside when I wanted to be a detective.

'This is ridiculous,' Yadi interjected.

'You're ridiculous,' Tati inserted. 'Nothing is more absurd than a child who wishes death upon his own father.'

'Here we go again,' Njet reached over to light the cigarette that Kik had set between her lips.

'You—' Yadi began speaking but Afif grabbed him before he could form another word.

'Keep talking,' Afif hissed at me.

'After that, I'd go over to her house as often as I could, usually around 1 p.m., when I got out of school, until 3 p.m., when Babaji was free to take us for a drive. After a month, she told me she wanted to help me with my detective work. I said that being a private eye was no easy task, that it was dangerous, for example—'

'A detective can't refuse to go into the Terror Castle, can't attack a mummy, can't run when a grandfather clock lets out a sudden noise, can't be afraid when facing a nervous lion?' Kik asked, finishing my thought.

'Exactly. I'm touched you know me so well, Kik.'

'You tried to give me the same excuses that you used to lie to an eight-year-old?'

'But you bought it.'

'I didn't buy it. I just didn't want to argue with you, so we could break up already.'

'Smart move.'

Njet put his face into his hands. 'Enough. Stop arguing. What happened with this girl?'

'She cried,' I said, clicking my tongue a few times. 'Back then, I thought that making a girl cry was a terrible sin, so I gave her a box as a way of saying sorry.'

It was Babaji who helped me come up with the idea.

The rules of the game were simple. We would write something down, anything at all. For example, 'I'm going to eat bread for breakfast' or 'My farts smell', but whatever it was, we would pretend it read the same way: 'You already know what I wrote.' It's a little joke, get it? Babaji thought it was really cute when I'd ask the girl, 'Hey, what did you write?' and she'd answer, 'You already know what I wrote.' Babaji suggested that I buy two black boxes of the exact same size so that the game would seem more mysterious. I couldn't find identical ones in black, so I opted for two different colours and covered them both in black cardstock.

When I gave the girl her gift, she was a bit confused. I explained the rules and added, 'It's a detective game. You can practise so that later you'll be a great private eye, just like me.'

We played the game from age eight to twelve, which is when we stopped spending time together.

'Thinking back to it now, Babaji's game was silly, paradoxical. The whole point was to pretend we knew something we couldn't possibly be aware of.'

My tongue flapped against my gums three times as I shook out a cigarette. I placed it between my lips.

'Oh, this reminds me of a different story,' Tati cut in. 'Back when my husband and I were dating, we also had our own private game. We came up with riddles about how different animals evolved. My husband would ask, for example, 'What species are okapis related to?' and then he'd count to 10, and I'd have to come up with the funniest answer possible, like: 'A drunk zebra crossed with a horse.' It's the kind of game that makes you believe in evolution without taking the whole thing too seriously. If time ran up, whoever didn't answer had to give a piggyback ride to the one who asked. That was the gist. After we got married, we played the game all the time, until one day I announced we needed to stop. I'd got a message from God. Darwin leads us astray with all his talk of evolution.'

I suppressed an urge to giggle and had the feeling that everyone else was doing the same.

'Can we get back to the black box?' Kik asked.

I lit my cigarette. 'Babaji left when I started high school.'

I needed a way to keep myself busy. Fixing up old motorbikes sounded like an interesting option. I flipped through some ads in the newspaper, and then I saw the one:

SELLING FOR CHEAP
Binter Merzy Motorcycle, 1976 Model
Not looking for money. Just a buyer with balls.

It's not that I had a death wish, but I desperately needed a hobby. I called the phone number listed and the seller asked me to stop by his garage.

Before showing me the merchandise, the seller insisted on recounting the story of how he'd acquired the bike. He didn't want me to buy a lemon, he said; he wanted me to buy a lemon together with its sour backstory so that I wouldn't complain if I ended up getting squirted in the eye.

'No one wants to buy after hearing this,' he said as an introduction.

The seller had got the bike from a friend whose old roommate was the most infamous motorcycle thief in Surabaya. No one doubted the thief's talent. It was rumoured that if he stomped his foot three times in front of your house, you and your entire family would fall fast asleep. And some said that he could switch on a bike's ignition with a simple snap of his fingers.

One night, the thief stomped in front of a house with yellow mourning flags outside. People were still on the porch making small talk after the recitation of the Tahlil, but all of a sudden, they fell into a deep sleep. Unimpeded, the thief entered the house, sneaking towards the garage to caress a motorbike that only hours before had sent its passenger to the afterlife. This wasn't the first time the two had met. The thief had tried to swipe the bike on six different occasions and failed at every attempt. The motorbike thwarted the thief's most expert strategies, and that irked him. This robbery wasn't about earning a bit of cash; it was a standoff between thief and motorbike. And when they met again that night, the thief had new tricks up his sleeve.

'Some say they were locked in struggle until the pressure of their bodies released a bolt of lightning,' the seller told me. 'Others are convinced that the combined strength of the motorbike and his thief raised the temperature of the earth, which is why Mount Merapi erupted over Yogyakarta that same night.'

The legendary thief triumphed and drove his prize home. His roommate was passed out on the couch. The thief chained up the stolen bike in the kitchen, then fell asleep next to his friend. The next morning, the friend woke up to the feeling of something wet dripping down his cheek. Half awake, he blinked open his eyes to the sight of his roommate's head smashed in. It took him a few minutes to collect himself before following the trail of blood across the floor. It stopped right in front of the motorbike's tyres.

The motorbike's original owner had been a street racer who had never once lost a competition. Rumours circulated that he'd made a deal with the devil, calling on a jinni to possess the bike—and not any old jinni either, but a Cheetah Jinni. In exchange, he offered the spirits part of his body, which is why he was missing the pinky on his left hand. His competitors were resentful of the racer's success and tried to even the playing field by placing curses on the motorbike. This angered the Cheetah Jinni, and the bike bucked its owner off in the middle of a race. The street racer careened into a road-side restaurant, his cheap helmet splitting in two. He died on impact. Less than 24 hours had passed after the death of his first owner before the motorbike took yet another life.

The seller looked me up and down. 'So. You still buying?'

I handed over a wad of cash, signed a waiver and took the motorbike home. I named the bike Cortázar, after the protagonist in Harahap's novel. Harahap, in turn, had named the character after his favourite author, Julio Cortázar.

While Babaji set out to start a carpet business, I kept myself busy with the task of training Cortázar. We were equally stubborn. It took us nine months before both of us gave up on dominating the other and decided to be friends. 'Then, one night, Cortázar rekindled my interest in the black box Babaji had told me about.'

A motorbike gang had been loitering on the curb, and Cortázar intentionally chose to gallop over one member's foot, which meant that the rest of them zoomed after us in hot pursuit. We had no choice but to hide, pulling over near an abandoned house by the side of the road. The gate was broken, so I concealed Cortázar in the bushes and scampered inside. I walked through the living room, then opened up the doors to all of the other rooms one by one. When I decided to go upstairs, I realized that the house wasn't actually empty. A person was standing half-way up the staircase, framed by a stained-glass window. The light of the moon filtered through the coloured glass, making the figure appear viscous. She was a woman and smelled like peppermint. 'Looking for this?' she asked, holding out a black box. I spun around and ran, or at least it felt like I did. As it turns out, I never left the living room. I'd tripped over one of the table legs and hit my head, and only came to the next day.

'It must've been a dream,' Afif offered.

'I sure hope so.' I stubbed out my cigarette. 'But whether or not my subconscious invented the whole thing, I realized that I'm haunted by the box, though I'm not sure by which one. When I went to university, I figured out that all Babaji had done was slightly alter Wittgenstein's beetle-in-a-box thought experiment for my childhood game and riffed on a Vaishnavist legend to come up with the story about Achal the farmer as a distraction for me while my parents fought. But the weird thing is, even though all of these stories are made up, I can't get the box out of my head.'

'This sounds like some nutjob obsession of yours, which means that you brought us here to satisfy your own delusion,' Kik said. 'But hold on one second—Njet, someone on the street keeps glancing in our direction.'

The mechanic slowly rose to his feet, glaring at me in a way that might've meant, 'I don't think I can be friends with someone like you,' or 'I'd like to stuff your head into a barrel of molten asphalt.' Or maybe I was projecting.

We heard a commotion outside. Yadi dashed towards the noise. Kik grabbed Koka from the table and ran after Yadi while Afif and I shielded Tati, who got angry because she thought we were making her look weak.

'Rules are rules. It's not my fault your car is busted. With an old clunker like this, I need at least a week to work on repairs, and for that, I need to see your ID so that I can keep the vehicle here without any trouble,' Njet raised his voice, confronting a guy roughly Afif's age, stocky and wearing a muscle tank that showed off a tattoo of a face split in two. The right half was reminiscent of a face on a totem pole, while the left resembled an old man kept out in the sun too long. In-between the halves of the face was another human head, sticking its tongue out. And above that, the letters *kwakwaka'wakw*.

Njet pointed at a sign on the shop's door. 'Want your car fixed? Give me a copy of your ID.'

'But I didn't bring my ID and I'm busy,' the guy replied. 'Come on, I've got places to be.'

'As it happens, that makes two of us,' Njet answered, waving us back inside the shop and leaving the kid to sulk on the street.

'You're wrong, Kik. This isn't just about me. Let me finish,' I said. 'Two weeks ago, I was driving around looking for an engagement ring for you and Njet. But Cortázar was acting up. He turned left when I wanted him to turn right, right when I wanted him to turn left, until finally he pulled to a halt just in front of a jewellery store. Clever Cortázar. I decided to look for a ring there, even though I was fairly sure they didn't carry the kind I wanted. A pretty woman greeted me out front. Later, I found out that her name is Nurida—that's your wife, Yadi. With a fake smile she said, "Welcome to Wan Ali Jewellers, where the majesty of heaven comes down to earth." It made me want to puke. And I'm pretty sure Nurida wanted to punch herself in the mouth for saying it.'

'Yeah,' Yadi agreed. 'We really hate that slogan. If heaven is full of stingy people like Wan Ali, I'd rather go to hell.'

That made me chuckle.

The stench of roses and some other intense fragrance assaulted my nostrils when I entered the store. It wasn't a nice smell, but the spray must've been pricey because it didn't make me feel nauseous the way cheap air fresheners do. Coincidentally, the day I went into the store was also the owner's 57th birthday. He offered me a brownie and a plump date. He didn't once drop the smile stretched across his face, even though his teeth were starting to rot.

'There, in the middle of Wan Ali's celebration, I spotted the black box that had haunted me all this time.'

'See? What did I tell you? He's delusional. Who in their right mind would ask all these people to chase down their personal obsession?' Kik said in a huff.

'Like I said, you're wrong. This is about a secret. Secrets, my dear friends, are little creatures that burrow into your brains. If you keep them up there too long, they'll eat you from the inside out. Better to just expose them straight away. And that's what a good detective is for,' I turned around clicking my tongue five times. 'As for why I asked you all to be here, you . . . ' I pointed at Yadi, square in the face. 'You need money if you don't want your wife to divorce you. And you two,' I gestured back and forth between Njet and Kik, 'you need capital for your business. Look, Wan Ali is too rich to spend all his money in the short time he has left on this earth.'

I tapped my tongue as I approached Tati, setting my hand on her shoulder. 'You've had a grudge against Wan Ali for some time, haven't you?'

She paused. 'But I'm not a bad person, not like you.'

'Oh, come on. No one thinks they're a bad person,' I said. 'Good people do bad things, then they excuse themselves for what they've done by coming up with an ethical motivation. You can justify anything. If you don't want to settle this grudge of yours, why don't you consider the robbery as an act carried out for the greater good of mankind?'

'I don't know what grudge you're referring to,' she said.

'Really?' I asked, click, click, clicking. 'I think you do.'

Tati fell silent. My tongue moved to the rhythm of a ticking clock.

'Maybe you've forgotten why you're so angry at your brother-in-law. But reflect on it for a moment,' I whispered into Tati's ear, 'your blood boils when you hear his name, and that anger is real. Wouldn't it feel great if the evil thoughts you wished on Wan Ali came true?'

Tati stared at me. I glanced at Yadi. 'How many times have you thought about torturing your boss?'

I turned my gaze towards Njet, Kik, and Afif. 'How many murders have you all committed in your head? How often do you fantasize about committing terrible crimes without having the guts to carry them out? Tomorrow, on March 4th, all of you are free to forget about sin. My job here is merely to assist you in transforming thought into action.'

'What about me?' Afif asked. 'I don't have anything to do with this. I don't fantasize about hurting people.'

'You . . . ' I worked hard to suppress giggles. 'If you really think what you just said is true, go ahead, walk away. The same for the rest of you. If I'm wrong, leave. Do I have to repea—'

The sound of an engine revving and cars squealing sounded from outside the shop. Njet grumbled, 'Just because he's a big dude he thinks he can do whatever he wants.'

'Hold on,' Kik hit Njet's arm, 'didn't that guy say his car was completely dead?'

'Maybe it started working again. You never know with junk heaps like that.'

Kik dashed outside as though something had just dawned on her. Not long after, she came back pale as a sheet. 'Koka's gone. He stole it.'

I pressed a finger against the tattooed shoulder in the image of the masked man on Afif's t-shirt, squarely beneath Afif's breasts. She slapped my hand away. 'What the hell do you think you're doing?'

'That's him,' I said, pointing at her shirt. 'That's who was just at the shop.'

—TRANSCRIPT V—

[Five minutes of silence, with some intermittent whistling.]

Look, I have no choice but to close this case. No choice at all.

[A door opens. Heavy footsteps approach.]

I want updates, Mr Double-Bind.

M-making progress, sir.

Give it a rest and let her go already. She's clearly not in her right mind. Talk to her long enough and you'll go crazy too. You'll see soon enough.

Respectfully, sir, most murderers aren't in their right mind.

It wasn't a murder. How many times do I have to say that to you?

I just need a few more minutes. I can prove it.

[Laughter] You know, if you're so opposed to admitting you made an idiotic mistake, you can just force a confession. Any means necessary. It'd be quicker.

B-but . . .

You want a promotion, right? Then play the game.

[Heavy footsteps fade. A door closes. Silence for roughly 20 seconds.]

Is your husband home?

Probably not, no one picked up. That's all right though. I haven't even had a chance to cook today because you've kept me here so long, officer.

Are you ready to tell me what I want to know?

Hm . . . what's that now? Ah, you must be referring to the robbery.

What? Which robbery?

The jewellery store I robbed. Well, me, in a team of five other people.

—END OF AUDIO FILE—

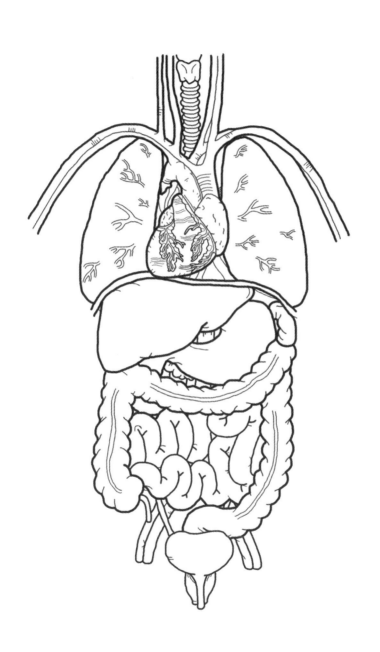

06

I'd rob the jewellery store with Afif, Yadi, Tati, Njet and Kik in 13 hours.

We were sitting at a warung that specialized in fried catfish. While waiting for our food, I ruminated over aliases. Fresh names always come in handy when crime is involved.

Tati's hand reached down to scratch at her ankles every few seconds. Mosquitoes swarmed the tent we were under, located right next to a pond. Everyone ordered something except for Tati, who claimed she wasn't hungry. 'You can skip dinner all you want, but never neglect breakfast, even if all you eat is a bowl of plain porridge.'

'Oh no,' Yadi shook his head. 'Here comes her healthy-living rant. She loves nothing more than lecturing people, and recently she's expanded her range of topics to include the afterlife.'

'You may have stopped living under my roof,' Tati said, 'but you mustn't forget to eat breakfast. People who skip the first meal of the day are at a higher risk for heart attacks, and that's a fact.'

Pongo was a good fit for Yadi, since his full name—Suryadi—was ludicrously gallant, while the shortened form made me think of a dutiful child, too soft-spoken to talk back to his mother. Pongo captured Suryadi's personality perfectly. I started to think that I should've been the one to name him at birth. If Yadi was to be Pongo, then Tati had to be Pingi. Pingi and Pongo. Complementary opposites, like Yin and Yang, darkness and light, day and night, and the quadrillions of other dualisms. Plus, if you say the names one after another between four and six times, without saying 'and' in-between, it sounds like you've said a phrase in Xhosa. I watched a documentary about daily life in Kwazulu-Natal and found the language people spoke intriguing. To my untrained ears, the clicks bounced off the other syllables like sounds from an old slot machine in an underground gambling hall hidden inside the building of an abandoned supermarket—resounding across the cavernous space. 'There's some truth in what your mom is saying. Back when I played kick volleyball—' Kik had started offering her opinion but Afif cut her off, impressed to learn that Kik had been an athlete. The young girl complimented Kik, saying that none of her friends was any good sepak takraw. I was taken aback, since my new friend had never once expressed interest in anything. During the few hours we'd spent together, Afif showed signs of being a very passive person. She reminded me of a goat that'd made its way onto a crowded lift at a shopping mall: it was obvious she shouldn't be there, but she wasn't able to leave because people were constantly shuffling on and off, shoving her further towards the back. I thought about giving her the alias 'Goat-Stuck-in-Lift', but upon further reflection, I decided it was too wordy. Agnes would have to suffice.

Kik smiled at the praise, waving away a mosquito before continuing. 'My coach showed me a study about the health benefits of a good breakfast. Apparently, people who skip the meal are more likely to suffer weight gain and memory loss. That's why it was mandatory to have breakfast in the dorms.'

I'd come up with the alias Kik when she and I first met. No need to mess with a good thing.

'You might think that's true,' Agnes said as she lit a cigarette, 'but I hardly ever eat breakfast, and look at my body. As for memory loss, that wouldn't bother me, but so far, your study doesn't seem very accurate.'

'Not yet,' Tati retorted. 'Back when I'd examine patients, I always asked if they regularly ate breakfast. Most said they didn't, and they were also white-collar workers. I read a different study showing that people who head into the office on an empty stomach are more likely to feel tired and sluggish in the afternoon. Their choices affect entire companies.'

Njet plucked the lighter from Agnes's fingers. 'I've also happened upon some health articles that back up what Tati is saying. But the thing is, all these researchers ask is whether or not you eat breakfast. That makes people think about what they eat, not what they drink, right? Nothing in the survey says, "Hey, do you drink water after you wake up?" Staying hydrated is as important as oxygen. I may skip breakfast, but I never forget to have a glass of water once I'm out of bed, first thing. My body feels great all day.'

I observed Njet's face as he spoke, trying to brainstorm a name that might suit him better. But Njet was the only option. He didn't deserve all that effort on my part, but we each needed an alias for everything to run smoothly.

'You're hungry,' Pingi said. 'You might not notice it so early in the day, but your stomach needs sustenance.'

'That's not the only issue,' Pongo stopped his mother. 'Have you heard about people who skip breakfast on weekends because they sleep through the afternoon, waking up right in time for dinner?' Pongo scratched the top of his head. 'I'm like that, and look at me, I'm big as a balloon.'

'Sorry, Pongo, I have to correct you there,' I cut in. 'Small balloons also exist, so it'd be better to compare yourself to the Seated Woman of Çatalhöyük.'

'What?' Pongo asked.

I scratched a bite above my eyebrow with my pinky finger and exercised my tongue, clicking a few times. Then, I replied with conviction: 'Not everything needs an explanation.'

Njet showed us what came up on Google. We laughed.

'How about you?' Agnes rested a hand on my shoulder, holding it steady even when I shot her a dirty look. She even met my gaze before finally releasing me. 'Any opinions on breakfast?'

'An important meal, one that helps us digest whatever we might've inadvertently swallowed in our sleep. Spiders, cockroaches, lizards and the like.'

A few in the group let out nervous laughs, massaging their necks.

Pongo started mumbling just a bit too loudly. 'Why won't she answer?'

'Who?' I asked. 'Your wife?'

No response. I assumed I'd hit the nail on the head. Pongo asked, 'In your guys' experience, what is someone trying to say when they ignore your texts?'

Agnes suggested that the person might be trying to come up with the best way to phrase how they feel, and when the message doesn't come out right, they have to type and delete and type and delete until finally they feel satisfied. Kik answered that the person is usually mad and doesn't want to talk for a while. Njet advised Pongo to call whoever it was, but Pingi disagreed: 'If Ida's the one who isn't replying, she no longer respects you as her husband. Get a divorce.'

I tried to offer another alternative. 'You want her to text you back? Hand me your phone.'

Pongo hesitated.

'I'd never take someone else's belongings by force, but I'd happily I use unsavoury methods to convince you to willingly give me your phone.'

Pongo rolled his eyes. He listed a few ground rules, all of which slipped my mind the moment his phone was placed in my palm. Bold of him to think he could tell me what to do.

I scrolled through his recent calls, which contained the following contacts:

'Pig-face' (a lot of people use animals they find cute as nicknames for their partners.)

'Hot mama' (maybe Nurida was 'hot' in Pongo's eyes.)

'Buttons' (I imagined this might be a contact for a seamstress Pongo had hired.)

'This is her, right?' I pointed to 'Pig-face.'

Pongo shook his head. 'That's Wan Ali's wife. Nurida is "Buttons".'

I did a quick double-take. He asked me, What? I replied, What, you call your wife 'Buttons'? Nurida's cute, like a button, he'd said, which I suppose was an acceptable explanation.

Okay.

I called Nurida. She picked up the fourth try.

'Hi, I'd like to get a text from you. Answer this, please.' I hung up and composed a pithy message.

Hey~ :3

She replied before I could toss Pongo his phone.

WHY DON'T YOU JUST CALL ME!!!

'I have a feeling Nurida wants you to call her,' I said. Pongo snatched the phone from my hand, hurrying behind the warung. Not very suave. I thought about the triple exclamation points Nurida included in her text, wondering why she felt so drawn to hyperbolic punctuation when a hundred exclamation points wasn't about to make her message more intimidating. But I had to admit Pongo seemed very scared.

It took us a mere 15 minutes to inhale the food that came to our table. When we were done, I told everyone that I'd prepared aliases for the group, that these names were for our own protection, and that from then on, and until a determined point in time, they should get used to calling each other by these pseudonyms. Pongo demanded why he had had to be Pongo, just like his mother, who complained about the name Pingi. I explained my reasons.

'Why don't you have an alias?' Agnes demanded, and the others backed her up.

'Me?' I asked with a flap of my tongue. 'I already have one.'

'What is it?' Kik asked.

'It's secret.'

'Okay then . . . ' Pingi leaned towards the others. 'What secret should the rest of us cook up while you refuse to tell us?'

I thought for a second. 'How about you just call me "Secret"?'

The question of names was trivial to them, so they didn't waste my time arguing. These fools wouldn't know danger if it looked them in eye.

We blew another 30 minutes on cigarettes and empty chatter. Njet, crazy as he is for construction, brought up proportions: Can the golden ratio really be found all over the universe? Was this design principle at fault for Jennifer Aniston and Brad Pitt's divorce? (Angelina Jolie's features follow the ratio perfectly.) Pingi, pious as ever, changed the topic to mysticism: prostrating oneself in prayer is required six, nine or 34 times a day, as per the number of times the word *sujud* appears in the Qur'an. Agnes, in typical form, challenged each of Pingi's statements with logical rebuttals. She took everything the old bat said too seriously. We would've kept it up all night had I not interrupted to suggest that the CIA might be recording our conversation.

We left the catfish joint at 12.16 p.m. We'd all have so much more time if humans didn't need to eat, but kicking back after a meal is so pleasant that it would be impossible for most people, me included, to give up the habit.

When we were ready, confusion passed over Pongo's face. He couldn't find his car keys. Pingi reminded him that Bachtiar kept track of his keys by hanging them from a necklace chain. An argument was unavoidable. If two Siamese fighting fish are about to brawl, the best course of action is to separate them. While Pongo scanned the ground and Pingi nagged, I went over to Cortázar and patted the rump of the bike, whispering: 'Don't be mad, okay?' Pongo finally found the keys in the dirt, right around where he'd phoned his wife. I asked him to hand them over and tossed him Cortázar's in exchange. Njet would ride with Pongo, and I'd drive Pingi, Agnes and Kik. This was the first time Cortázar would run without me.

Pingi took deep breaths throughout the ride. Her wrinkle-encrusted eyes seemed fatigued. Regret doesn't have to be expressed aloud, you know; bodies speak for themselves. She started quietly humming a lullaby over and over again, and by the fourth or fifth refrain I'd got the lyrics and melody stuck in my head. I'm not sure what was going through her head, but I had the feeling that if I'd started singing along it would've interrupted her train of thought. Instead, I composed an accompaniment of tongue clicks.

My love for you
stretches wide as the earth to the moon
from moon to Medan
and then down to Honolulu

I want to make
Myself multiply
Five billion times
So I will love you
Five billion times more

Tiny buttons, easily lost
Big buttons can trouble make
Little ones who curl up at night
Grow up without shame
I can teach you a skipping game
Tomorrow morning when you awake

She sang until she drifted off but woke up when I suddenly slammed on the brakes. Some crazy sedan sped past us, grazing Cortázar. Cortázar fell. Cortázar never falls. Cortázar can't fall.

We all rushed out of the car. The night air was mercilessly chilly. Smoke rose from the remains of a garbage pile still smouldering by a nearby park, and the faint smell of burned plastic hung in the air. The driver also stepped out of his vehicle. He was wearing a pink mask snug against his face, which exaggerated the egglike shape of his head. He pointed Koka at Pongo and Njet. When Njet removed his helmet, the man reacted as though he'd made a mistake: he lowered the weapon and helped push Cortázar upright. I calmly walked in their direction.

'You better have an explanation for this, Pink Porpoise,' I said, slipping one hand into my pocket.

Never gets old. 'If not, you won't have much time left to say anything at all.'

Out of the blue Agnes sprinted headlong towards the man and hugged him. She turned to me and asked if I had a marker or a pen handy. Kids these days.

'That man who paid me a visit earlier today,' Pingi said. 'He's very kind and considerate in both words and actions. Nothing at all like you.'

'He looks like the guy who stole Koka back at the shop,' Kik chimed in.

'Yes, the one with the weird tattoo. You know, he does look pretty similar,' I took a few steps towards the man and whispered, 'Hey, Porpoise, let the girl go.'

The masked man struggled to release himself from Agnes's grip. 'Hurry up,' I said, still calm. 'I rarely lose my temper, but when I do, you really don't want to be the reason why.'

I knew that hugging Agnes was never his intention, but I was enjoying the position the situation put him in. Agnes let go. As my fanatic friend walked past me, I saw her tearing up. Why was this so important to her?

Pink Porpoise aimed Koka at me. 'I'm the one who gives the orders. Quit it with the chitchat and get back in the car.'

I strolled in his direction, hand in pocket, while Njet got up from the ground and hit the masked man from behind. Unfazed, he grabbed Njet by the arm and held Koka to his head. Pongo ran to Pingi's side and Kik took cover behind me. 'Go on, keep walking if you want to push me to extreme measures,' he said. 'Or do what I say, and I'll let your friend go.'

'What is it that you want me to do, exactly?' I asked.

'I told you, get back in the car.'

I could hear Agnes and Kik whispering. Njet looked as though he was trying to communicate something with his eyes. Unfortunately, I was at a loss for what. I tried to brainstorm fifty ways this might play out in my favour, but I only came up with one: an uppercut to the masked man's jaw.

'No use lying to me either. I've been following you for months,' the man reached into his pocket and pulled out a photo of me getting dressed. 'Here's proof.'

First, this guy makes Cortázar fall. Then, he holds a gun to my friend's head. Next, he claims to have shot this half-naked photo of me. Finally, and worst of all, he has the gall to think he can tell me what to do. My mother is the first and last person whose orders I ever followed.

'I know you don't like this,' the man added. 'The last person you took orders from was your mother. "Doing what I'm told? That's what made your father leave me." She said that to you that, didn't she? And ever since you haven't thought twice about doing things your way. But this is different, you might end up making a mistake you'll regret.' He was pressing Koka harder and harder against Njet's head. I hoped Njet's cranium was as strong as Ade Rai. 'I don't want to repeat myself, Gaspar.'

This guy was serious. He knew how to imitate the way I would've spoken and acted, were I in his position. I put my hand up, the one that had been shaped like a pistol under my jacket. He'd got my attention.

Pongo shuffled to my side and whispered, 'You must have heard about kidnappings before, right? All you need to do is trade something in exchange for the hostage. I have no clue what's going on between you and this washed-out rock star, but it doesn't look like he wants cash. I think you should do what he says.'

'You're not wrong,' I whispered back, then smacked my tongue against the roof of my mouth for one loud click. I raised my other hand. 'It's your lucky day. I'd rather no one get shot tonight, so let's have a chat.'

—TRANSCRIPT VI—

Are you willing to state on the record the names of your five accomplices?

Of course, of course. Other than me, there was Pongo, Njet, Kik, hm . . . hold on, I'm forgetting this one. Agnes? Yes, if I remember correctly, her name was Agnes. And the last one was Secret.

You realize you aren't in a position to be hiding anything from me right now.

No, n—oh! It's all coming back to me, the most unusual thing happened to us when were on our way to the store. Do you remember that man we were talking about earlier, sir? He held us up, and he had a weapon. Oh my, officer, I'm sure you've experienced all sorts of things like that in your line of work.

That—

[Static for 20 minutes.]

—END OF AUDIO FILE—

07

Less than 11 hours to go, and Cortázar, Afif, Yadi, Tati, Njet and Kik were all on board for the heist. Right on schedule, were it not for the masked lunatic who got in our way. Time to wrap this up.

'How'd you end up so skinny, Gaspar?' he asked me. 'Or should I say, Budi Alazon.' The masked man smoothly struck up a conversation once we'd entered the car, preventing me from distracting him with my own digression. 'It wasn't easy for me to get as built as you used to be. And here you are now, scrawny.'

In a low voice, he continued. 'I trace your every move. I know your dreams, I know your fears, I know the words you wish would come out of other people's mouths. The words you miss. I know it all.'

'Wow. Stop wasting my time, Porpoise,' I said. 'You have 15 minutes to tell me what you want so I can get on with my plans.'

'All right. I-I . . .' he said, stammering. 'I'm a bit nervous, to be honest.'

'Then get out of the car and do 100 push-ups. That's what I'd do.'

'Really? How do I not know that?'

'You only know what's in the news. And frankly, what I've said in print should stay there.'

He shook his head. 'I know more than you think. I also have this.' He showed me an old notebook titled *My Days*. I penned that volume, Budi Alazon's journal, in the style of Hitler's *Mein Kampf*. How this stranger had managed to get his hands on it was a mystery. Showing interest with a question, however, would compromise my position further.

'I've done everything,' he said. 'I eat what you eat, drink what you like to drink, make a living by arm wrestling. I haven't skipped a thing.'

'You ate the roaches?'

He nodded. 'I even finished what you never could: I beat Minesweeper. I documented my victory, just to show you.' He pulled up the screenshot on his phone. 'You didn't die, I was sure of it. I can't explain how I knew, maybe there's a special bond between celebrities and their fans. I started searching for you, and here we are. But now I find out about push-ups as a coping mechanism, which never made it into the book! I should've started a long time ago.'

'Enough,' I interrupted. The guy was freaking me out. 'Get out of the car, do the push-ups. Then we'll talk.'

'Only 100?'

Dammit. I should've said a higher number.

While the masked man's torso pumped up and down on the pavement, I thought back to those days when everyone decided to leave me. As you already know, my parents were content with their new families. Any emotional bond that once linked us had already dissolved. I wasn't angry at my father or his new wife, they didn't see me as family, nor I them. But then Babaji, the one person I felt close to, also left. He went off to try his luck as a rug salesman.

I was fully self-sufficient by my 16th birthday, and it was a lonely and frightening way to live. The freedom to do whatever I wanted with no one looking over my shoulder came with a heavy solitude. Imagine dragging a coffin filled with shallots across an empty beach, not a single sunbather on the horizon. You can sense the waves lapping the soles of your feet, teasing you. You might kick them away, but waves always come back, it's in their nature. The beach, an open-air prison of limitless sand, devoid of mountains or landmarks on which to fix your gaze.

When I was 19, I was informed that my father died of a stroke. I went out to the driveway and gave Cortázar a long bath, explaining as I scrubbed that we were about to get a lot of money. 'What do you think we should do with it?'

Cortázar carried me to Uda, a used bookseller who never revealed his real name. Books can keep loneliness at bay, he told me, so if I didn't want to feel alone, the best thing to do would be to open a reading room. A brilliant idea: no one wants to seem dumb these days, and knowledge of books is a surefire way to seem smart, so a reading room must be a great place to make friends. I blew a chunk of my inheritance on all of Uda's old books and magazines. He filled his truck with a collection of around four thousand volumes and deposited them at my doorstep. I hired a few workers to transform my garage into a comfortable space and designed some flyers. Everything would be free: coffee, snacks, instant noodles. Visitors could do whatever they wanted, even steal the books, so long as they showed up. I spent all of my time in that garage, listening to Motorhead as I ate, falling asleep reading fiction. That's when I became obsessed with Huracán Ramírez, the legendary Mexican wrestler I learned about in a collection of sports biographies. I started crafting my own lucha libre masks. Only five people had shown up at the reading room in the three months since opening day, so I had loads of spare time, enough to draw the designs myself and take them to a seamstress. Soon, I'd abandoned the dream of bringing people together and focused on building muscle mass.

One day, the bass player for Slank, Bongky Marcel, stumbled upon the reading room. He'd seen Cortázar outside and wanted to compliment me on the bike—not an unusual reaction. But after checking his reflection in the motorbike's side mirror, he walked into the refurbished garage and promptly fell asleep. Eventually, when he woke up, Bongky explained what was going on. He'd just spent five days alone near a fishery outside of Sukabumi. It's pretty stressful, playing bass, he said. He made himself a coffee and checked out the space for the first time. Whoa, this could be a dope recording studio, he added.

We introduced ourselves, and he told me all about the music scene, a world I knew little about. By the time he'd left, I'd already decided to donate my collection of books to local schools and renovate the space yet again, this time into a recording studio. I wasn't a musician, really, but I'd been blessed with a so-so voice and more than enough guts to stage dive off a tower of amps stacked two metres high. I hired a studio operator and recruited some kids from a nearby music school to complete my band. I want our sound to be like Motorhead's, I told them, and decided I'd wear one of my lucha libre masks on stage. My name would be Budi Alazon.

This is about when I got into coke. Every bump felt like riding a roller coaster with no safety bar. Slack-jawed, I kept doing lines, scent sharp like a women's perfume, until my nostrils were slashed. The dust sucked up the moisture in my throat and I'd feel like 400 neon lights were shining into my eyes while a tarantula crawled around at the back of my mouth. I can still feel the thrill of those spider legs on my tongue even 10 years after I got clean, those beams of light glowing every time

I hear the drug's name. It refused to let me go, just like the ghosts of my family members. They've tracked me my whole life: take a deep breath and you'll catch a whiff of a decaying body. Always, at every turn.

Call me a spoiled child, an addict, think what you please. But if you've never felt what it means to be truly alone, to end each day with a heaviness that makes you want to rot in your own bed, then I'd prefer you keep your opinions to yourself. Everyone thinks a junkie is a junkie is a junkie. That's all talk, not a finger lifted to help. When you try to get clean, people stare like you're a walking corpse, a useless shell of a human being, which doesn't give you much choice but to fall back on old habits. Crack helps you get perspective, but it won't fix your problems.

Once, I was sure I was about to die. Not from an overdose, from *something else*, but the feeling is the same. Cortázar rushed me to a 24-hour clinic, but they didn't have the facilities to treat me, and I had to be transferred to a hospital. Lying on my back, who-knows-what-drug pumped into my veins. I felt great, but the conversation the doctors started having by the side of my cot made me nauseous. Why didn't they talk somewhere else, where I wouldn't have to listen to them? Thinking about it now, of course, I realize they'd done nothing wrong. They assumed I was unconscious, if not well on my way to death.

When the doctors left the room, I was desperate to leave. Still loopy, I tried to remember where Cortázar might be. The bike doesn't ride well after he's been left on his own for too long. Finally, after bouncing my tongue up and down seven times, it occurred to me that Cortázar must be waiting in front of the clinic. I hailed a cab.

Cortázar and I cruised down a long, quiet street. One or two other motorbikes sped past us. The glow of their taillights snaked into the distance as though they were racing the rising sun. Dawn broke, people started going about their days. They're all sons of bitches from the moment they're born, I told Cortázar. Anyone who thinks differently is at best delusional and at worst a liar. People only seem good when you think about them in hindsight, or when you imagine them in the future, or when you picture that someone who's just out of reach as you drift to sleep. If that person is right in front of you, standing by your side every step of the way, you have three options: you get bored, you hurt them, or you get bored and you hurt them. Then, I explained how long, long ago these concepts human beings call love and empathy really existed; you could cradle them in your arms, even kick them across the ground. Then, one day, a tidal wave wiped everything out. What we understand to be love and empathy today are mere legends, half-dead and fossilized in language.

Cortázar hit the gas until we were careening at over 100 kmph. I thought about distorted mirrors. My face felt warped, as though I was staring at a hot air balloon when confronting my reflection. There's not a single being so powerful as that, not even God. Face such a twisted version of yourself and you'll realize that ugly distortion is capable of anything, no mercy, not a single soul spared. Then the thought of Cortázar's former owner came to mind, and it occurred to me that I might die that night, though I'd prefer my head stay intact. But nothing happened. Cortázar slowed to a stop near a warung, and the old man who worked there served me a cup of palm wine and told me about how he'd travelled from Luiqiçá, in Timor-Leste, all the way to Bandung before ending up in Jakarta. I listened to his stories until I fell asleep on the bench, only waking up when I rolled onto the dusty ground. I chucked my Budi Alazon mask into the trash, on top of some empty bottles and cigarette butts.

'Done daydreaming?' The Pink Porpoise had gotten back in the car, steadying his breathing. 'Look, I need you out there with me tomorrow. They miss you.'

'I don't miss them,' I said. 'Even though it sounds like you do. By the way, I like your take on my mask. Your design?'

He nodded. 'I sewed it using the instructions in your book.'

'I included that?' I wondered aloud. 'Beats me what made it through editing. Anything embarrassing?'

'No,' he answered, 'well, except for some passages about love. You wrote, "Love is about who sticks around the longest." A bit cringey.'

144

I chuckled, waiting for the image of someone's face to surface in my mind, but I drew a blank.

'Fine,' I said. 'Maybe I'll come. But—'

'Trust me, that *maybe* of yours could kill one of the few friends you have.'

'You're serious about imitating me, aren't you?'

'You need to be there tomorrow.'

'Fine, but only if I don't die today.'

'What exactly are you planning?'

'Something risky,' I said. 'I'd love to say more, but sadly, I only reveal secrets to friends. This conversation would look different if we you were making an effort to become acquainted with me.'

'But I *am* you. Friendship's irrelevant, compared to that'

'Sure, you may have modelled yourself in your image, but the thing is, I'm not sure I trust myself. I need friends, confidants.'

'Consider me a friend, then.'

'You don't get it. You have to work at it, not just call yourself a friend. Those are two different things. And this would require that you be yourself, not me, when you promise to keep a secret. As a friend.'

He took off his mask. 'Is this enough for you? Or are you also going to ask for my ID?'

'That'll do.' I took a deep breath and announced that I'd confess to why I left the music industry. 'I was recruited by the CIA,' I said proudly. 'Now I investigate human trafficking rings.'

'Bullshit,' he laughed. 'You think I'd believe that?'

'If you believed me, I wouldn't be a very good spy. In any case, it's a deal, I'll be there tomorrow. Since you know me so well, you should feel confident that I'll keep my word.'

'You've broken promises before,' he replied. 'Twice.'

'Well, this won't be the third.'

'If you don't show up,' he said, tone threatening, 'I'll hunt you down, and when I find you, I'll drag you across asphalt at full speed in the afternoon heat.'

Incredible. It was like I was having an argument with myself. I borrowed one of Agnes's catch phrases for my retort: 'If you say so. But keep in mind that no matter how precisely you copy me, you won't have any say with Cortázar. That bike has free will.'

'Can we be done here?' he asked, but his tone was polite.

'Happily.'

He left the car. I considered calling out to him and clarifying that Budi Alazon and I were not the same person. Sure, I was the man behind the mask, but the rock star had his own backstory: he grew up on the streets, made a living arm wrestling, and even ate live cockroaches. Fiction, all of it. He's the protagonist of the novel I started but never finished, that I might never finish.

Someone once told me that fiction has to make sense, unlike reality. Budi Alazon failed in that measure, so why not make him exist in a real life? The world doesn't need another logical story.

I paid off the members of my band to spread the rumour of Budi Alazon's death based on the plotline I'd composed. They exaggerated, but by that point the narrative was out of my hands. I didn't have it in me to break my fan's heart, having seen his zeal up close. Budi Alazon died that afternoon in a burial of bottlecaps and cigarette butts, but Porpoise had dedicated a lot of energy to becoming the rock star's spitting image.

I leaned against the bumper and waved Pingi, Kik and Agnes into the car. A stray dog circled my legs, rubbing against me. I casually strung together a haphazard explanation about what the guy wanted, concluding with a chuckle. No one seemed to believe me, but they didn't ask for any more details. I scooped the dog from the ground and moved its front paw up and down, like it was waving goodbye. Pingi shot me a disgusted look. Of course she'd think dogs are impure. I, on the other hand, think strays are amazing. Just imagine how they got all their scars.

Pongo offered to drive the car. I have no idea what happened with everyone else while I was talking to Budi Alazon II—not that I care—but somehow Pingi and Pongo had stopped arguing. They were on the same team. It reminded me of what Sun Tzu wrote about *shuai-jan*

147

snakes, those tricky buggers from Chang Mountain. If you attack the snake's head, it hits you with its tail, and if you attack its tail, it strikes you with its head. If you attack it in the middle of its body, the snake retaliates from both extremities. Quite the long-winded story just to communicate that it's wise to keep a united front. I hopped on Cortázar, and Agnes was perched behind me by the time I fired up the ignition.

We'd barely travelled 10 metres before Budi Alazon II's car made a U-turn and cut us off again. He handed over Koka and asked me if I'd nabbed the shirtless photo. I shook my head, adding that he better not jerk off to that picture. He dug around his pockets, scanned the asphalt, and even stopped the Starlet, insisting everyone get out of the car before finally leaving without having found what he was looking for. More time wasted.

Agnes was unusually quiet as we drove. Maybe it was shock, the huge Budi Alazon fan that she was. Time to brainstorm a word to describe going-mute-after-meeting-one's-idol syndrome.

Pongo beside us, and Kik leaned out of the window to ask where we were going now. I called back that we were headed to Wan Ali's store. Pongo hit the brakes, and I didn't have any choice but to follow suit.

Pongo stepped out of the car. I walked over and explained: 'Some reconnaissance, that's all. We need to take a look around, make sure that everything will go as planned.'

'What on earth do you need to check?' Pongo demanded. Kik, Pingi and Agnes had formed a semicircle outside the car, and Njet joined them. 'Does anyone here know what's going on?' Pongo asked, and everyone shook their heads. 'This guy,' he spat, sticking his finger in my face, 'he's twisted. The reasons that brought us here are deranged. I don't think he has a plan at all, and we're all going to end up hurt. Have you heard about the devil? About temptation?'

'Don't point your finger like that,' Njet interjected. 'I don't care if he's Satan himself, that's plain rude.'

'Rude? Fuck you.' Pongo shoved Njet to the ground, then straddled the mechanic's skinny body, lifting his fist to punch him.

'Friends,' I quickly interjected. 'We've all told a lot of stories today, but have you heard the one about the insular cortex? Loyal and brave Tristan from the story of Tristan and Isolde had an insular cortex. That's the part of his brain that made him die from suffering. Battle wounds, those he could withstand, but he couldn't take it when grief started eating away at him.'

'Is that your idea of a threat?' Pongo asked. He got off Njet and stalked towards me.

'Is that what it sounds like?' I asked in response. 'Pongo, all I'm trying to do is share a story with you, like you so often do for us. Tell me, can you picture what Nurida's face looks like when she wakes up in the morning?'

'Of course I can, dumbass.'

'Then I suggest that you tuck that memory away carefully. Because if you don't make peace with Njet right now, I'm going to drive away with the rest of the gang. You'll stay here and you'll stay poor, which means Nurida will divorce you.' I clapped Pongo on the back. 'All I'm doing is looking out for that insular cortex of yours.'

Pongo extended his hand to Njet, still on the ground, and offered an apology.

It was 1 a.m. when we finally arrived at the warung next to Wan Ali's store. I pulled the iced-tea bottle from my bag and drank a swig of its contents before setting it down on the bench beside me. The man running the place was asleep. Agnes, who wanted to buy cigarettes, woke him up and the two of them started chatting in Sundanese. Njet and Kik were bantering over by Cortázar; watching them, I could tell it was a lot of fun to flirt with someone you're dating. I'd have joined their conversation, but they looked happier than two bears that had just escaped the circus. I'm not one for optimism, but still, I hope they stay that way, at least until the kid turns 18. After that, I couldn't care less if they start fighting and end in divorce. Pongo and Pingi were in the car. The faint sound of Pongo laughing while his mother smoothed his hair drifted my way. Cars occasionally drove by the warung, casting their lights into the distance before speeding out of sight. A scavenger swung their hook into a trash heap; they fished out a plastic bottle and added it to the sack slung across their back.

Budi Alazon's mask likely met a similar fate. The scavenger walked past me and, smiling slightly, asked if they could pick up an empty bottle under the bench. I shifted my legs to one side and inhaled the sharp scent of the scavenger's body. It reminded me of spoiled milk, dry sweat or blood. Maybe a combination of all three. The scavenger smiled again before vanishing behind a truck parked on the curb. A hand waved in front of my eyes, trying to catch my attention.

'The man who works here says you also came by yesterday.'

I nodded. 'Should we dispose of him to make sure he doesn't snitch?'

Agnes smacked me. 'You wouldn't dare,' she snorted. 'What were you thinking about?'

'Concocting new criminal acts,' I said quickly. 'I suddenly got tired of my immense capacity for evil. I could transfer it to someone else, what do you think?'

'Sure, sure . . .' she said. I didn't like her tone. 'Whatever.'

'I'll get a great night of sleep once we pull this off.'

'We?' She laughed. 'This is your plan. You won't tell us what we're about to do or how we'll do it. All we've done so far is follow you around for hours.'

I tried to steer the conversation in a different direction. 'What were you and the owner talking about?'

'Nothing much. I used to live in Bandung, which answers your question from earlier about Sundanese, and as it happens, he used to work in Bandung, even though he's from Timor-Leste. He grew up in Garut, so his Sundanese is really fluent. I can barely keep up.'

She laughed. I clicked my tongue.

'He also told me you come here all the time,' Agnes added. 'You must've really planned this out.'

'I'm the villain, aren't I? I have to chart out the perfect plan,' I answered. 'It needs to go without a hitch. That's why I wanted everyone here at the jewellery store early, to get a lay of the land.'

'Why this obsession with the black box?' she asked. 'What's really so special about it?'

'I could answer with a long list of qualities if that's what you really want to know. You heard what Pingi told us, and from Babaji's story.'

'You don't believe all that, do you?'

My tongue thrummed against the roof of my mouth.

'That's a strange way of laughing,' she said. 'Reminds me of someone who helped me out when I was in a bad place.'

Agnes grimaced, grasping at her chest. At first, I thought it was a bad joke, but then her body went limp.

'Hey, Pongo!' I shouted. 'Make that hulking body of yours useful for once and come help me carry Agnes to the car.'

Pongo awkwardly jogged over, layers of fat bouncing. I was a bit worried he'd be too tired to pitch in.

'Nothing to worry about.' Pingi placed her ear to Agnes's chest when they reached the car. 'Most likely a very mild heart attack, but it looks like she'll be fine.'

Pongo, exhausted after carrying Agnes, stumbled over to the warung and grabbed the iced-tea bottle from the bench, gulping down its contents until he started coughing and tears spilled from his eyes. He complained that his throat was on fire. 'What is this, gasoline?'

'Calm down, you're not going to die. It's absinthe.'

'Absinthe?'

'Oh wow, it's your first time. Let's just say it's a pleasant beverage,' I said, lighting a cigarette. 'Congratulations, you're now a fully realized person.'

Pongo stuck a finger down his throat and threw up. But there was nothing he could do; absinthe is clever at hiding in your body's crevices and sticking around for a while. Eyes red as berries on a coralwood tree, he gazed at me as though possessed. In a frenzied voice he said: 'You son of a bitch.'

I chortled until my stomach hurt. The others laughed too, except for Pingi. She massaged the back of her son's neck.

'Where'd you put the copy of the keys?' I asked Pongo. Still shaking with anger, he told me he'd left them in the glove compartment. 'Go get them,' I replied. 'It's time to poke around the store.'

*

Pongo was the one to collide into a trash can, one he tried to kick, and missed. Pongo was also the one to comment, 'I've never seen that kind of flower before,' pointing to a used tissue discarded in front of the roll-up door, 'What a nice touch!' After I'd managed to open the storefront, it was Pongo who politely knocked on the door and called out hello. Pongo was the one to abruptly announce that he felt a special kinship with Chuck Norris. Finally, I located the light switch. When the space lit up, I was the one to call out, 'Good evening, Wan Ali.'

Pongo turned to run like a thief caught in the act, but I grabbed him by the collar. Stay calm, that's what I told everyone. 'This is all going according to plan.'

Wan Ali had been sleeping on his favourite couch, locked in an embrace with his black box. He rubbed his eyes and, at the sight of the five of us, instinctively grabbed a broom leaning against a nearby wall. 'Get out!'

'Not to worry,' I said. 'We'll be leaving shortly.' I walked over to the jeweller while smacking my tongue against the roof of my mouth, then pressed Koka into his belly. 'Of course, we'll be back to rob your store in just about,' I glanced at my watch, 'that's right, just about 10 hours from now. We stopped by to say a quick hello to you and your little box.

'This weapon of mine holds a bullet that can easily puncture your stomach lining,' I continued. 'What did you have for dinner?'

He tightened his grip on the broom handle. 'T-t-tati? Yadi? What are you doing here?'

Both of them were quiet, but I felt like it'd be rude not to offer some explanation. 'They're with me, robbing you.' I handed him a photo. 'Tell me what you and your wife were saying about the people in this photo before we played chess for the first time.'

'W-what? I don't know, I . . . I forget.'

I clicked my tongue in four rhythmic beats as I waved the photo of Bachtiar back and forth in front of Wan Ali's face.

—TRANSCRIPT VIII—

[Static]-teresting. What next?

The two of them were in the car for a while, maybe half an hour. My leg fell asleep. I said as much to Pongo, I'm always complaining to him. He grumbled but walked with me to one of the park benches. It was very dark. What do park service employees do with their time, I wonder? All the lampposts were broken except for one, and it was at the opposite end of the park. It was chilly, so Pongo offered me his jacket. He started walking away, but I asked if he wanted to stay and sit with me. I didn't want to be alone.

What happened in this conversation?

I asked if Pongo recalled the incident of August 20th, the day his father taught him how to ride a bike without training wheels. He fell and broke his baby toe. We hurried home so I could give him stitches, and because he was crying, my husband told him a story about the bravery of Belka and Strelka, the two Soviet space dogs. Pongo told me he remembered.

No, not you two. I'm asking about the others.

How should I know? They were in the car.

The victim never mentioned anything?

No one felt the need to discuss it. Njet was safe, and we went on our way.

So, nothing else took place.

Well, a stray dog went over to the boy you're calling the victim, which means he must've been a good kid. I didn't approve of how he picked the dog up, but I'm fairly sure dogs are excellent judges of character.

And the altercation ended, just like that.

Yes. What did you expect? A shoot-out?

What next, did the masked man leave?

Yes, he had to get ready for a concert.

Concert?

That's what I said. Did I forget to mention that he's a musician? I can't remember what name he goes by, but he seemed famous.

Budi Alazon, maybe?

Yes, a complicated name, just like that.

I had a feeling this masked man might've been Budi Alazon, based on your description, but I didn't want to rush to conclusions. The man's a legend, an idol, and three days ago, he headlined in a concert after 15 years off the scene. It's all too odd to be a coincidence: this man who attacked you called himself Budi Alazon, performs in a concert, and within 24 hours, the victim dies under suspicious circumstances.

Maybe it was an offering to the jinn. He wouldn't be the first person to have dirty dealings with evil spirits in exchange for fame. I wouldn't be surprised if you searched his house and found red candles or jars filled with placenta. Besides, there's no such thing as a coincidence, officer. God has a plan for everything.

[Sound of a throat clearing.]

Say, how might God plan a murder?

Careful, sir, or you might not get that promotion.

I couldn't care less about the rat race. I want this to be a clean case, solved without resorting to those slapdash methods my supervisor's so fond of.

I think you've been very professional, sir.

Get this through your head: your opinion doesn't matter. Your only job is to tell me who murdered that kid.

I have no clue what you're talking about.

You were called down to the station to give me some answers. And right now, it's time for you to state everything you know, no dilly-dallying.

I'm only capable of describing what I remember, officer. As an upstanding citizen, I believe in cooperating with the police.

Are you trying to make me suspicious? You constantly talk in circles, like you're hiding something.

Be patient, sir. You're young, but your blood pressure could rise any day now. I had this one patient with a heart condition, and he—

I don't give a damn. [Sound of a fist slamming down on the table.] I want to make myself very clear. The body was found three days after time of death. An autopsy indicated that cause of death was a heart attack, but there was foul play, I knew it the moment I saw the corpse. You and your so-called friends spent that entire day with the victim. Before we locate the others, and before that autopsy report is filed, I want the name of who did it. You're claiming that you and your friends met this rock star, but none of it adds up: he had a concert the next day, wouldn't he be busy getting ready? Maybe this is your way of throwing me off your trail, adding a new suspect to the mix. You've been trying to slip things past me from the first question in this interrogation. And you think that being old means I'll take your word for it, just like that. Do you have any clue who I am? I graduated top in my class at the police academy. This bit of yours might work on those fat-asses out there, but not with a detective like me. Look at my chipped front teeth. You know how that happened?

It seems unnecessary to point a gun at me like that. I'll probably be dead in a year or two, just wait. And I don't understand how your class rank or whatever happened to your teeth has anything to do with this investigation. I'm not here for your life story.

[Static for two minutes.]

Excuse my behaviour, ma'am.

You're excused. Don't worry.

I'll level with you. I can tell that you're a good person. Honest. The kind of person who has no intention of ending up in hell, isn't that right?

Na'udzubillah min dzalik.

And you haven't had the chance to feed your bird today, I'd imagine?

No, I haven't.

All right then. Those are three excellent reasons for you to give me the short version of what happened. Feel free to skip right to the part about the murder.

If this is how you're going to act, I don't see how you're so different from the other detectives.

You know why I'm different? Because right now, I'm about ready to lodge a bullet in your skull if you don't quit rambling. [Sound of a pistol cocking.]

You're possessed.

If there's an evil spirit in this room, it's you.

[Silence for roughly one minute.]

Okay, I just remembered something.

What? It'd better be important.

Wan Ali confessed something.

What did he say?

Wan Ali, he's gone mad, just like my son. He had the gall to claim my husband died, right after a meeting with his business partners. It makes no sense, of course. If you ever meet Bachtiar Abdillah, you'll see what I mean. I've never known a man in better health.

Wait. This Wan Ali character is your brother-in-law, right? The one who owns the black box you keep going on about?

That's right, and after all that drama with the masked man, we went to Ali's store. To do some reconnaissance before the robbery.

You stole from your own brother-in-law?

That bothered me at first. I'd tagged along because I was nervous that my son would crash my husband's car. Bachtiar adores that Starlet, and then it turned out they were going to commit a robbery, targeting my brother-in-law's store, no less! I knew it was wrong; at any rate, I'm aware it's a sin to take someone else's property. But then I thought about it more and realized there wasn't anything wrong with what they were doing. I've wanted to teach Wan Ali a lesson for a long time. I can't remember what he did, but I hate him so much, to the point where I'd gladly watch him suffer. Again, I can't recall why, but that feeling of loathing is so strong that a robbery seemed justified. Plus, he's so rich that he almost certainly insured his store. It's not as though all his money would disappear with a little heist.

Go on.

Are you sure you want me to? This isn't a simple explanation, and most of what I know is based on words Wan Ali said to save his life. He made his confession under duress, so he constantly went on tangents as a tactic for buying time. Besides, my stories seem to annoy you, officer.

It's fine. Yes, I'm annoyed, and I've heard more than enough bullshit for one day. But there's no way I could stomach filing a report on this interrogation. So why not, talk as much as you want.

That's music to my ears. Here's what happened. That night, we snuck into Wan Ali's store, and when we turned on the lights, we found Wan Ali sleeping on the couch. He woke—[static for two minutes]—stuttering, Wan Ali told everyone what happened between him and my husband.

My husband had gone out one night, saying he had plans with an old friend. This is all thanks to Facebook, make no mistake. Haven't you heard? That evil technology designed by the Jews is to blame for how people act nowadays, at least according to the news stories I read.

Then my brother-in-law described what happened next. He, my husband, and Maimunah met up with Sir Shakur's son, I mentioned him earlier. My husband is a skilled businessman and an experienced manager, so Sir Shakur's son asked him to join a new venture, something to do with his family's scrap-metal business. My husband asked if he could bring in Wan Ali, since my brother-in-law is good with people, then Maimunah tagged along. Up until this point, the story rings true. But then Wan Ali claimed that they'd gathered to go over profits made from ransacking metal from Singaporean ships dumped off the coast of Jakarta, as well as from the wreckage of malls burned to the ground during the lootings in the north zone of the city. I'd never heard a peep from my husband about business plans like these. That's where the lies started.

Next, Wan Ali confessed that as they drove home, all the four of them could talk about was what they were going to do with the stacks of cash they'd made off those dirty dealings. As my husband saw it, they should all donate half the profits to the Chinese people targeted in the lootings. They'd profited off scrap metal scavenged from Chinese neighbourhoods in distress. Wan Ali is a clever storyteller, he knew my husband well enough to make the whole thing sound plausible. He claimed that he and Maimunah disagreed with Bachtiar. They wanted every cent of profit they'd earned with their own sweat and blood. If you want to make a donation, go ahead, they'd said, but not from our cut. Wan Ali paused to cry. 'Forgive me, Tati,' he snivelled. 'Forgive me.'

He continued: they'd been driving down a quiet street lined by rice paddies, and in the heat of the argument, my husband crashed into a parked truck. Wan Ali and my sister left him there, stuck inside. The truck driver stumbled on the sight of what had happened as the sun rose, right before dawn prayers. He called for help the moment he saw the smashed little car. They tried to get my husband out, but he was pinned against the steering wheel, already dead. They even had to cut off one of his legs to free his body. Meanwhile, Wan Ali was left with a broken hand, Maimunah with a sprained toe.

How could I believe such a tale? None of it adds up. My husband was with me yesterday. Sure, he went out this morning to meet up with that old friend of his, but he'll come home later this evening.

You also said your husband had gone out to meet that friend three days ago . . .

That's right. You're starting to pay attention. Three days ago, my husband went out with his friend, and the same thing happened today.

In other words, your husband never came home.

No, he was there last night. This morning he left again, but he'll be back.

And if I'd asked you this yesterday, let me guess—your answer wouldn't change. But enough—

Oh, who cares. Yesterday is yesterday, today is today. That's how it works. It doesn't matter if my words are the same, the meaning changes with the passage of time.

Hold on. It just occurred to me, but those lootings Wan Ali was talking about happened in 1998, right?

Of course, what else could he have been talking about?

[Laughter from the police officer. Silence, followed by laughter from the witness. Then, static for 18 minutes.]

—END OF AUDIO FILE—

CORTAZAR

Kawasaki Kz200—'Binter Merzy'

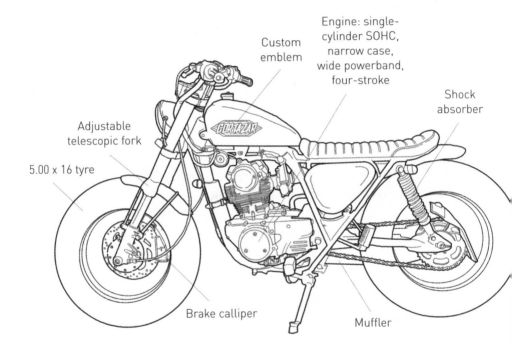

Custom emblem

Engine: single-cylinder SOHC, narrow case, wide powerband, four-stroke

Shock absorber

Adjustable telescopic fork

5.00 x 16 tyre

Brake calliper

Muffler

A Cheetah Jinni possessed the body of this 1976 Binter Merzy, and as a result, the motorbike has free will. Additionally, Cortázar enjoys music, especially songs by Chrisye, and sprays motor oil to mark his territory. His other hobbies include growling loudly in the Pasar Minggu tunnel in South Jakarta—the acoustics make his snarl all the more alarming. As a result, the motorbike is a popular topic of conversation among truckers carting vegetables to the district's market.

08

Pongo lost it. He started punching the air and then grabbed Wan Ali by the neck, shouting *murderer*, *asshole*, and *you're about to pay, motherfucker* over and over. Wan Ali begged for forgiveness as Njet, Agnes and Kik attempted to peel Pongo off the scrawny jeweller. Pingi stood silently by the door, toying at the hem of her shirt, mouth opening and closing as though she was singing, but without making a sound.

'Take it easy, Pongo,' I said. 'No more strangling for now. Wan Ali has more explaining to do.'

The four of them spun towards me at the exact same time, as though asking in unison what other possible sin this rancid old man could've committed. 'About the box . . .'

Agnes pried the black box from Wan Ali's hands and tossed it in my direction. 'You're still hung up on your goddamn obsession after what he told us? That's rich. I hoping you'd be capable of doing one thing that would make me respect you.'

'I don't need your respect, Agnes. And for your information, I wasn't talking about *this* box'—I kicked the box back in her direction—'but a different one.'

'Asshole. What "other box"? How many could there possibly be?'

'That's a ridiculous question,' Njet snorted. 'Didn't you know, Agnes, that the Earth itself is shaped like a black box? And Gaspar's balls stack one on top of the other like units in an apartment complex.'

Pongo sprung forward, lunging once more at Wan Ali's neck and grasping it like you would a cassava plant. The insole of Kik's foot struck Pongo's left ear before he had a chance to see whether there really was a starchy vegetable somewhere inside Wan Ali's throat.

Pongo collapsed. Wan Ali gasped for air.

'He knows what I'm referring to,' I said.

'How much have you snooped, you cursed boy?' Wan Ali demanded. Kik yanked the cord from the broken fan and used it to tie Wan Ali's hands behind his back.

'Just a bit. I found out that you had the heart to leave your brother-in-law alone, sandwiched against a steering wheel, bleeding out. I also learned that you sold your pre-teen daughter to a wealthy paedophile, justifying your actions in the name of God. And she also died in a pool of blood, in her case from blunt trauma to the uterus,' I spat out. 'I bet one or two items on that list should be enough to land you in prison.'

Ninety per cent of people go about begging for mercy in the same way, and Wan Ali was no exception. I took a tape recorder out of my backpack and pressed record while Wan Ali confessed everything about how he and Maimunah had left Bachtiar to die. Sending the file to the police wasn't a bad idea, but I'd come up with more interesting options. 'I'm going to lock you in a room and find a stereo that can play this confession on loop. I'll feed you, of course, just enough to keep you alive, listening. Maybe I'll add some magic mushrooms to the mix to help you visualize the events of that night.'

It was an empty threat, obviously, just my way of spicing up the investigation. 'Or we keep this in the family and resolve things a bit more amicably. What do you say?'

Wan Ali nodded.

'Well, then.' I held the tape recorder against his lips, pressing Koka hard against his abdomen. 'Tell me what happened to your daughter.'

Wan Ali's mouth formed a trembling smile, then he spit on the floor. 'I see, you're this detective friend Kirana was always going on about.'

Pingi, who had been silent all this time, approached Wan Ali. 'It's been a while since I've heard any news about your daughter, Ali. Since she got married.'

'She's dead. Deceased. Gone.' Wan Ali tilted his head back, like he was remembering something. 'That damned old man. He was the one who did it, he killed her.'

'Still blaming others, Ali?' I asked. I felt pressure building in my throat, creeping towards my head. 'You're the one who did it. You forced her to marry one of your business partners at age twelve. Twelve! She hadn't even had her first period. Fuck, you deserve to be locked in a room with Hitler and Suharto, forced to listen to their self-justifying bullshit for the rest of your days.'

'Nonsense. As a good father, it's my duty to marry my daughter off when the time is right. It's not my fault that she found her match at such an early age. I gave them my blessing, for the good of them both.'

'Great,' I said, making my tongue do push-ups as I selected the most damning words I could string together into a sentence. But I was at a loss. What was the point? 'Respectable people' like Wan Ali make me sick. Their invocations of morality to defend every action they take make me sick. Better to burn everything to the ground than squabble over good and evil.

'Listen to this, "good father",' I said, loosening my lips by flapping my tongue for two more clicks. 'I saw Kirana a month after she got married. She asked me to help her, lifting her skirt to show me the blood and pus between her legs.'

She was too scared to say a word to her parents. At that age, the only advice I could muster was to line underwear with tissues and wait until I could figure out what was going on. 'I get it now. You, the scum of human civilization, search for religion only to dig up anything that'll justify desire and wealth.'

Kik was staring at me. I imagined she'd be crying, since she's always tearing up over something. Agnes and Njet looked at me too, mouths agape. Pongo grunted from where he was lying on the floor. Pingi patted me on the shoulder and whispered something in my ear, but I couldn't hear what. I thought about how, somewhere, a chameleon was crawling along the branch of a mango tree in someone's backyard, dropping its eggs, which would eventually hatch on the ground, and then the baby chameleons would crawl out of their shells and rush back up the trunk. I was a lot like the unlucky guard dog who kept watch over the whole thing.

Wan Ali's lips moved like a toilet seat. Open, close.

I marched over to the dark purple box with its delicate flower pattern, lying on the shelf between souvenirs from Mecca. A long time ago, Babaji had helped me cover a similar box in black cardstock. Resting above it was a photo of a little girl, smiling.

Wan Ali was quiet. He watched me turn the box over in my hands with a pathetic look in his eyes. I explained that no one was here to punish him. To be haunted by guilt is a fate worse than a biblical flood or the plagues of Egypt. Stammering, Wan Ali swore over his late daughter that he would safeguard the life of every individual present if I didn't send him to prison. I flatly answered: in prison or not, he, his wife and everyone in that room would rot soon enough. 'All I want is to take a close look at the contents of this box while drinking a cup of hot, sweet tea. Better yet, with some kastengel and biscuits on the side.'

Njet and Kik jumped in with statements about justice, which would've sounded more compelling were justice synonymous with martabak Melabar prepared with eight duck eggs, a delicious snack whose plump shape brings joy. Or if justice were a concept that, the moment you cut into it, releases the aroma of ground beef and chopped green onions. But none of that has anything to do with our widely accepted definition of 'justice'.

Fuck it. Purple box in hand, I left the store. But when I got outside, all I could do was hold the thing, unable to muster the courage to look inside.

*

Someone patted my shoulder, and I felt my heartrate accelerate. Agnes's perfume. 'Let's go for a ride.' Agnes's voice. Cortázar wobbled, almost tipping to the ground.

'I told you, never sneak up on me from behind.'

She apologized and set the black box on Cortázar's seat.

'It's a nice offer, thanks,' I replied. 'But not now.'

'It wasn't a question. It's an order.'

'You know you can't tell me what to do.'

'But Cortázar can,' she said. 'Right, Cortázar?'

There she was, talking to a hunk of metal. Went mad, so it seems. I shook a cigarette from my pack. 'I'll have a smoke first.'

'Go ahead, while we're driving.'

'It's dangerous to smoke on a motorbike. What if an ember flies into the eyes of the driver behind you?'

'No one's on the road at this hour,' Agnes replied.

'What about ghosts?' I flicked the wheel of my lighter. 'As you know, spirits are just about everywhere. We're always bumping into them.'

'If you say so. But a ghost won't go blind because of stray ash.'

'What about—'

'I'll knock your head in with your helmet if you keep arguing.'

'That's what I was going for,' I said, tapping my head with my hand. 'Come on, hit me.'

She actually did. 'Now get on Cortázar.'

I hit the ignition and asked where we were going. Agnes asked if I knew of a nice spot to smoke. Anywhere, I answered. She repeated her question with emphasis on the word *nice*, and the only place that came to mind was the park where Budi Alazon II had intercepted us.

After four blocks, we drove by a bus stop shaped like a cassowary bird. The structure had become a choice spot for pigeon shit. Then we rolled past two houses separated by a two-metre fence. Both abandoned. I'd been inside those houses before. The size of the rooms and even the furniture was identical, with the exception of the layout in the guest bathroom. Agnes held me tightly as we drove, pressing her face against my back. I could feel the shape of her nose. 'What the hell, did you fall asleep?'

'I'm awake.'

'Good,' I said. 'You know you're not allowed to touch me from behind, right?'

'Yep.'

'Well, I discourage physical contact in general. Not to mention hugging.'

Agnes made snoring sounds.

We reached the park and Cortázar stopped by the fence. The stray dog, whom I often call Bin, came over to me. He always appeared like that, as though trotting from another dimension to arrive at my feet. I lifted him up, held him out in front of me, and asked in dog how things were going. He barked twice. I introduced him to Agnes; he barked again. Then, when I asked him to lick my nose, he said, still in dog, that he really needed to pee. I met his gaze and asked him politely to please refrain from pissing on Cortázar—in dog, of course—but he didn't seem to understand. He went over to Cortázar and lifted his leg. Our communication could use some work.

Agnes felt the need to talk. 'I guess you come here a lot. Or do you live nearby?'

I didn't answer, lighting my cigarette. 'You have a heart condition.'

She also changed the topic. 'You don't know how happy it made me to meet Budi Alazon.'

'Yeah, that kid is really something,' I said. 'Makes sense that you like him.'

'It's not that I'm a fan, exactly . . . how can I put it? Back when I was little, I needed a hero. You know, other kids like Superman or Power Ranger for the same reason. Everyone's looking for that feeling of being protected. Also . . .'

'What?'

'I guess he was my first crush.'

'Sounds like daddy issues.'

She swatted at my head, a gesture that roughly translates as 'don't act like you know me'.

'A photo of Budi Alazon I ripped out of *Trax Magazine* was my talisman growing up. You've probably seen it, it's that one where he's posing with his arms over his chest, showing off the tattoo on his bicep, the one with that weird design and some nonsensical text.'

I tried to stay quiet, but I felt the urge to somehow respond to what she'd shared. My honesty would've hurt her, and only cruel people kick others when they're down. So, instead, I laughed and laughed until I keeled over. It's an expression of joy, people say, and joy is meant to be good.

'And now, I have a new photo of Budi Alazon to covet, and in this one he's both shirtless and maskless. Sure, his body isn't what it used to be, but the tattoo doesn't lie.'

'Long ago, Eagle and Seabird descended to Earth and shed their animal skins to take human form. Then, Seagull, Killer Whale, Brown Bear and the King of Ghosts joined them, also as men. These ancestors of ours had to fight a league of giants, cracking their skulls in with axes and sledgehammers. Once the giants had been wiped out, they built a village and started to till the land. But it turns out that one of the giants had managed to survive, hiding behind a nearby mountain. He threw a stone the size of its eyeball over the ridge and then sunk into the depths of the earth. The stone hit Brown Bear, who suddenly began acting strange. He screamed, his eyes rolled back into his head, and his hand reached out to grab an axe. He swung at Seagull's head, then picked up a sledge-hammer and hit Eagle and the King of Ghosts, until they all joined the brawl. Killer Whale and Seabird were killed. Seagull died slowly, losing blood. The spontaneous rampage was the first war in human history.' I took a drag of my cigarette and exhaled the smoke through my nostrils. 'Their heads were battered from the blows, and with those wounds, something in their minds shifted, and whatever it was got passed down from generation to generation, eventually reaching us. Violence has been with us for centuries.'

'Budi Alazon knows that legend,' Agnes said. 'It inspired the tattoo.'

I focused on clicking out the beat to 'On Melancholy Hill' by the Gorillaz while Agnes smoked. There wasn't

anything left to say, and I would've been better for everyone if Agnes had agreed.

'You never had your eye on that black box, did you?'
Agnes said, tapping the purple box still in my hands. 'So
why not just open it?'

'That box . . .' I cleared my throat. 'It's filled to the
brim with evil. If I open it, who knows, everyone might
suddenly slit their neighbours' throats, if they don't lift
the knife to their own necks first.'

'If you say so, but—'

'Here's the thing, Agnes. Wouldn't you still like
mankind as we know it to stick around, at least for a few
more hours?'

'Not particularly. C'mon, open it.' Agnes rested her
chin on her hand while observing me. 'You're scared,
aren't you? Admit it, it'll be our little secret.'

'In my experience, those who never get scared end up
eaten by bears.'

Agnes giggled for so long that I grew worried she'd
choke.

'I'm bored of doing bad things,' I said, selecting an
unsettling topic to make her stop laughing. 'If you'd like,
I could ask you to take over those responsibilities.'

'Forget that. All I want is for you to open the box.'

'I crafted a doll out of red clay once, back when I was
a kid,' I told her. 'I really wanted the doll to walk and talk,
so I pretended that she could, and in my imagination, she

hit my dad. That made me mad: 'I didn't bring you into this world for you to do stupid things like that.' I left the doll in the yard as a punishment. The next morning, she was gone. I'd convinced myself that the doll really was alive, that she ran away because of what I'd said. After that, I chose each word I said carefully, out of fear that I'd cause someone else pain, and as a result I barely said anything. I really believed every tiny thing I said had the potential to hurt someone, no matter how thoroughly I'd thought it through. And then I met Kirana. She knew how to make me talk; no matter what I said, she'd laugh.'

Agnes imitated my clicking noise.

'As I grew up, I learned that there'd been a heavy rainstorm the night I left my doll outside. Babaji told me that years later, when I recounted the story of my sad, runaway clay friend.' I laughed quietly. 'That was around when I'd decided to thank Kirana with something more concrete than my free. Babaji said that girls like dolls, but not ones made out of clay. Dolls that have hair, that smell nice. I asked Babaji if he would help me find a doll; we ended up getting a stuffed giraffe. I liked it and thought Kirana would too. We went over to her house, but when we got there, she was in tears. That's when she showed us what happened to her. I panicked, grabbing a box of tissues from the side table, and told her to put all of them up her skirt. Just then, a man around Babaji's age called out to her from the other room—*honey*—and ordered her to go upstairs. Babaji and I sat in the living room until we got the message that Kirana wasn't ever coming back downstairs. So, I set the stuffed giraffe on the couch and left.'

'Then what?'

'What do you mean?'

'What led to the obsession with Kirana's purple box?'

'You're kidding,' I said. 'Who wouldn't want to know someone's innermost thoughts?'

'But now all those secrets are in your hands.' Agnes tilted her head to one side. She was so young; standing next to her made me feel like I'd aged a hundred years. 'Why not find out?'

'Good question,' I said. 'I'll think about it.'

She held out the black box. 'Come on, at least the evil one?'

'Fine. Open it.'

We looked each other in the eye, then opened the box.

*

Driving back to Wan Ali's store, I reflected on what I'd seen inside the box. The memory made me think of the unfortunate dog from that one Club 80's music video, in a humane society, meeting the kid forced to wear a bumble-bee costume from that Blind Melon clip, all while an Ita Purnamasari song—the one with the line that goes 'swallowed by time'—plays softly in the background. I forget what it's called, but I remember the chorus. I hummed the tune in my head, imagining that 'time' took material form, like Godzilla, a creature capable of swallowing up anything he chooses, even love. I couldn't hold back a laugh and belted out a slightly modified version of the chorus.

'My love for you won't change, not even if it's hit by a rock'

Agnes giggled behind me. She rested her chin on my shoulder and we shouted out the line again and again until reaching our destination.

Njet and Kik were sitting at the warung. They waved their arms and called out to us as we approached. Pongo was asleep in the car, Pingi humming some song she'd made up.

'That psycho insists on investing in my auto shop,' Njet said. 'And Pongo is now the proud owner of Wan Ali's store. Do you think his wife will still want to divorce him after hearing that news?'

'She better not.'

'Let's bet on it.'

I went over to the car, opened the door and placed my mouth right above Pongo's ear, then burst into song: 'My love for you won't change, not even if it's hit with a rock.' Pongo jumped, slamming his knee against the dashboard. To sooth him, I asked, 'How did it feel, imbibing the nectar of the gods? Any nice dreams?'

He cursed me out with passion.

I advised everyone to go home and rest, since we'd be robbing a jewellery store in eight and a half hours. That's just enough time for a good night's rest. The next day, we'd rendezvous at the warung. Kik chimed in, asserting that the robbery was already over. She proposed we all get together the next day to celebrate our success. Let's have a drink and chat, she said, adding that it'd be her treat. A tempting offer, but if we were going to follow the plan, the robbery would still need to take place at noon, I reminded her. Kik resigned. 'Whatever, it's up to you.'

Cortázar's engine rumbled to a start and we all got ready to leave. Agnes, behind me, asked if I wouldn't mind giving her a lift to the main road. She'd catch the bus from there. There I was, prepared to take her all the way home, but I decided against it. I had no clue where her house was, but the mere thought of a long drive made me tired. Pongo would drop off Njet and Kik, but as Cortázar went on his way, I noticed he was following me instead.

I dropped Agnes off and she waved goodbye. I kept driving, and Pongo kept following me, which made me feel like a police officer leading a motorcade.

Finally reaching my house, Cortázar rested on his kickstand while I turned to confront the Starlet. 'Are you guys planning on following me when I go take a piss too?'

Pingi climbed out of the car to hug me. My neighbour, the one who liked to tease me for never bringing girls home, was exercising in her yard. She saw this and smiled. Shit, she probably thought I'd finally managed to meet someone. The whole thing made me uncomfortable.

The car drove off and I stepped into my yard, locking the gate behind me. Too tired to open the garage, I asked Cortázar to park in his least favourite spot: the driveway. It'd been laid out before I was born; grass had started climbing through the cracks, consuming patches of pavement. Cortázar despised it; he'd fallen there several times. Forgive me, Cortázar. I was so tired, I needed to sleep at least three or four hours before finding my way to the concert. I lumbered towards my room, looking down at the purple box I hadn't stopped holding. What could Kirana have written? Maybe I'll open it, after I wake up.

—TRANSCRIPT VIII—

—lked about this. I had quite the scare once, before I retired. I'd stopped working at the hospital, I was already quite old by then, but I ran a little clinic out of my house. The hospital was so far away, after all, and I couldn't kick the habit of helping people. One night, a man came in and said he'd felt a sudden pain in his chest after having a cup of coffee. I could tell the boy had consumed something much stronger than coffee and readily spotted the trace of white powder on his nose. Cocaine. That wasn't so out of the ordinary in those days. Now, I can recognize a heart attack when I see one, and that's unquestionably what the boy was going through. But it was odd: the heart is on the left, and this patient was gripping the right side of his chest. Then, he told me he couldn't breathe. Ah, how could this have slipped my mind? His was such an unusual case.

The boy moaned and wouldn't stop tossing from side to side. His fingertips were going blue and the whites of his eyes turned yellow. I was worried, so I called my husband over, telling him it was time to drive the boy to the

hospital. There, the results of an x-ray baffled the doctors. The boy's heart was located on the wrong side of
his body. We stood around the cot, observing the patient
as we discussed his condition. He didn't have very long
to live, determined; no way he'd make it to 40. An innocent surprise, someone sneaking up on him from
behind—any of that could lead to an untimely death. We
all went for breakfast, and by the time we got back to
our patient, his bed was empty.

The tale of the boy with the misplaced heart spread
rapidly around the hospital. Some doctors were convinced we'd made the whole thing up, a sensational story
to get attention. Others who'd read about similar cases
in foreign countries were quicker to believe us, and they
soon the case was well known at other hospitals across
the city.

**Dextrocardia, that's what it's called, right? There are
more and more cases these days. I heard about someone
who was born with all of their internal organs reversed.**

Yes, and back then we had less information. The patient's
very existence became an urban legend. His condition
was delicate, and countless factors could have sped along
his death: surprise, exhaustion, excess emotion of any
kind, even joy. But that's only what the doctors and I
hypothesized when we treated him; cases like these
require a lot of research. I hope someone comes up with
a treatment.

Huh, interesting. But, let's get back on track. What happened eight hours later?

Pongo and I gave Njet and Kik a ride to the warung. We got there early, just before noon, but by 1 p.m., Agnes and that kid still hadn't shown up. We decided to swing by his house. It was quiet, and his motorbike was parked in the driveway. We thought he must've been so worn out that he overslept, so we celebrated our triumph over Wan Ali without him.

The next day, while my husband was out with his friend from high school, I took up Pongo on his idea to pay the boy a visit. When we arrived at his home, the front gate was still locked, and that motorbike of his had toppled over, sprawled on the uneven pavement.

—END OF INTERVIEW—

UN 4F1F

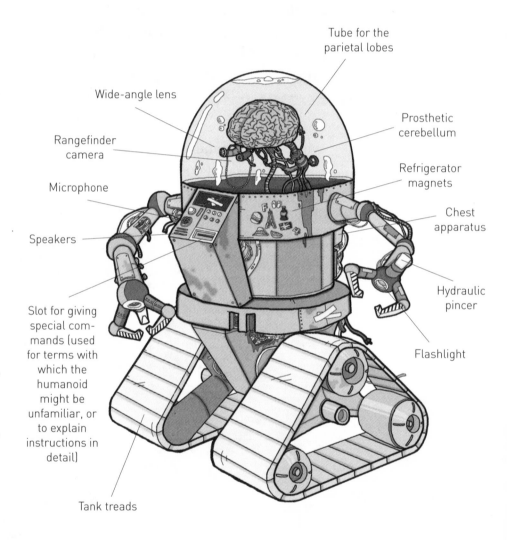

Tube for the
parietal lobes

Wide-angle lens

Prosthetic
cerebellum

Rangefinder
camera

Refrigerator
magnets

Microphone

Chest
apparatus

Speakers

Hydraulic
pincer

Slot for giving
special com-
mands (used
for terms with
which the
humanoid
might be
unfamiliar, or
to explain
instructions in
detail)

Flashlight

Tank treads